Mountain Magic

WAILING WICCAN

Jakki Frances

For my wonderful Willa muse – HEIDI.

You'll always be my favourite witch.

2020

PROLOGUE

"AAYEEEE!"

A screech echoes through the mountains. The moonlight casts a silver glow over the bush, reflecting off the rolling predawn mist. Bats twit as they dive and arch through the night sky, hunting the last of the small creatures before sunrise chases the nocturnal animals back to their warm, dark hiding spots to sleep the daylight hours away.

"AAYEEEEE! WHYEEEE? YAEEE!"

The keening continues, the call loud and tormented. Cracking as it rises and falls. On and on. Over and over the cries ring out. Eerie and mysterious, an indescribable sound. A sound that reverberates through the trees night after night. A dark, shadowy figure drifting through the undergrowth, moving slowly as the mist swirls at her feet. Seeming to float, a ghost moving slowly through the silver night. Searching. Crying. Night after night the strange being walks the mountains, keening. The genesis of many tall tales, ghost stories passed through the community around campfires in the dark.

Every night she was compelled to roam, crying, calling to those she has lost. By the predawn hours, her voice is raw and failing when she collapses into bed, only to repeat her nighttime ritual again the next. Only on the days surrounding the full moon each month was she given respite from her torment. Under the bright silver glow, from the night before to the night after the full moon, the persistent desire to walk the night eased. Giving way and allowing her the peace to rest and reconnect with her community. Month after month, year after year, the night called to her just as she called to those lost.

Frozen in time, she faced an eternity of wailing. Immortality stretches before her, such is the life of the wailing woman. The life of a banshee.

1991

CHAPTER 1

Willa huffed in frustration, throwing her bag into the corner as she stomped through to the kitchen. Rifling through the refrigerator and then the cupboards she searched in vain for something, anything, alcohol-based. But to no avail. There would be no artificially altering her mood tonight, her bad day was just going to have to sort itself out the old fashioned way. A relaxing bath and an early night in bed worrying and overthinking her life.

She hadn't been sleeping well. Plagued by the same dream over and over again. Each time she woke in a cold sweat, struggling to catch her breath and calm her racing heart. Every time she eventually drifted off, the dream returned to torment her. As dawn broke Willa gave up on hoping for restful slumber, opting instead for a large, strong coffee. At least there was a tangible reason for the rapid pounding in her chest and the buzz of awareness brought on by something other than magic. She could pretend that the coffee was the stimulant in her morning and not the unsettling understanding that the dream was no ordinary dream and felt suspiciously like something magical. Something was coming…

It was the voice more than anything that unsettled her… But then the dream itself was no more than a voice. The haunted, low cry, floating on the air. Over and over, a heart-wrenching wail seemed to echo through her mind, bouncing back on itself. AYYEEE! The heartbreak behind the cry was so clearly audible, Willa was unsure if it was the sound that brought tears to her eyes as she woke or the lack of restful sleep.

Willa knew the voice. She'd never heard it before, but it drew her in with such a feeling of recognition that she knew it was something, someone who would change her world.

Work had been the usual. Hours requiring laser-focused attention bent over her computer adjusting formulas a little here and there and then recalculating the entire thing only to go through the entire process again. Thanks to the exhaustion catching up with her, together with the persistent distraction of the voice that echoed in her mind all day and a stiff back all combined to induce a headache. All the tweaking and micro-adjustments to the latest formula assigned to her meant that any progress on perfecting the drug had been a complete bust. If she was completely honest with herself she wasn't surprised. A degree in chemistry, although sounding impressive, didn't really equate to anything impressive. Creating medications, no matter their use, wasn't nearly as exciting as it seemed in the movies. She'd never wanted to study science in the first place but her father had insisted. Her grades in school had been high enough to get her into pretty much any university course she chose, but all she'd ever wanted was to become a beautician. Her dream was to open her own little beauty parlour, spending her days chatting with people while doing their nails and giving facials. Her parents, however, had other plans. A high intellect was not to be wasted on something as pedestrian as beauty. Their goals for her were higher. She was to study medicine, law, finance or a science of some sort. Her father had degrees in International Politics, Global Economics and Engineering and had worked most of Willa's life for various high powered companies and occasionally Governments the world over. Travelling from country to country, advising on industry, security and international policy. All while Willa and her mother stayed tucked away safely in Australia, enjoying a quiet suburban life.

At her father's insistence, and under the threat of no funding for any further education whether it be university or beauty school, Willa undertook a science degree majoring in chemistry. Over the long years of study at university, any interest in chemistry Willa may have held was slowly washed away. Now, her school days were over. Now, she had a degree she had never wanted, in a field that she had no interest in and she would spend her life working for chemical companies, pharmaceutical companies and power companies. Spouting enthusiasm, groundbreaking ideas and impressive hypotheses that may one day become a life-altering medication, a cancer cure, a non-addictive analgesia… Something cheap to make that would be the drug of the century and make millions. All she really wanted was to sink below the fragrant waters of her bathtub and shut the world and her family out.

At least she had the weekend ahead to rest, daydream about a life away from a computerized lab, or at least get some laundry done. Maybe she'd rediscover discover her spark if she carved out some time to dabble in her kitchen, mixing herbs and oils, creating pleasing scents for the soaps she liked to make.

Then, of course, Sunday night was the first night of the full moon. A night to be spent outdoors, dancing and singing under the silver glow. A night for spell casting and wish-making. A night to celebrate the heritage her tight-laced parents denied; handed down from her grandmother. Willa's grandmother Ella was a Wiccan. A witch who practised the old pagan ways, worshipped mother nature and had taught Willa the magic she herself had inherited from her ancestors. And so it was, dating back through time, an unending chain of witches. Each generation taught their craft to the next, the young learning from the old, the young tweaking the magic and making it their own. This was how the Wiccan world developed. Spreading from far away Ireland centuries ago, to cross the ocean and arise in a new world. It combined over the years with the local Aboriginal culture, adapting to the new seasons, moon cycles and land until the day that Willa turned thirteen and Ella began her instruction.

Willa's mother had avoided learning even the basics of Wicca, denying their maternal magic, preferring to live her life human and ignoring the existence of the supernatural community that thrived in Australia. There was no room in the life her parents envisaged for Wiccan magic.

Undeterred, Grandma Ella had taken a confused, teenage Willa under her wing and into her home every school holiday. Spiriting her into the mountains and teaching her the ways of the Wiccan. Over the weeks of the summer break, she learned spell casting, winter was for studying the moon and learning to tap into its power. Springtime holidays were spent in the company of others - shifters, Fae and Aboriginal medicine men; learning each others histories and magic. The shifters taught her how to sense the particular flavours of others magic, to be strong, determined and forceful in her spell casting… And how to sneak out of the house after Ella went to bed. The young Aboriginal apprentices shared the secrets of the bush - what plants when combined made for good magic and which worked well for curses… And which when brewed just right could get you drunk quicker than any spirit purchased from the bottle shop. The Fae spent time teaching her to wield natures magic, grow plants, control the elements and add coloured highlights to the tips of her white-blonde hair. In return, Willa shared Ella's spells and recipes with her friends and encouraged them to venture into the human world for a movie, shopping trip or a sneaky night of mischief in a nightclub.

The full moon was something Willa had worked to keep sacred through the years. It wasn't always possible but whenever she could manage she headed back to her friends on the mountain for a night of magic and dancing, unfettered by the need to hide from the everyday human world around them. Their group had grown over the years as the supernatural community expanded through the mountains. New magic joined as old magic moved on, the supernatural community had always been very transient by necessity and remained so to this day.

But before she spent n night under the stars singing and dancing and sharing magic, Willa would spend her weekend cleaning and cooking for the week ahead and dabbling with her fragrant oil collection… She was in the mood for a new soap, something dark and spicy, something to match the idea of the perfect smell she'd been dreaming of for months.

"It's a big group tonight, what's the go?" Willa greeted Ella as they linked arms and strolled through the trees. The moon shone like polished silver overhead in a clear sky decorated with a million glittering sparkles. The large fire at the centre of the clearing kept the large crowd warm. Most supernatural beings embraced the less is more theory when it came to clothing, luckily their bodies also tended to run a little warmer than humans, combatting the lack of warm covering. Shifters were bare-chested or in their animal form, Fae preferred light sleeveless clothing to allow freedom for their wings, a handful of Aboriginals were dressed in traditional animal skin wrappings. The Wiccans were thoroughly covered in comparison, with long, flowing gowns that swept the ground as they danced.

Nodding to the far side of the fire Ella indicated a group, Willa's eyes widened taking in the four newcomers who were currently chatting with Dornan and Aine, a Fae couple whose young daughters were currently flitting around the glowing flames like brightly coloured fireflies. All four strangers were tall, slim, as pale as the moon and absolutely stunning.

"Vampires?" Willa gasped.

Ella nodded and steered across the clearing.

"Their coven just moved here in the past month, the first we've had here. I don't know much, yet, but I have heard they are mates. Who goes with who? I'm not sure. I guess we'll soon find out." Ella's murmured explanation was barely audible over the singing and chatter but the group of gorgeous faces that turned in their direction at her words indicated that the legends of vampire hearing were based in fact.

"Let's go and welcome them to the 'neighbourhood' and you can pump them for information." Willa giggled.

The quartet made an interesting sight even without their stunning looks. The fact that they were all fully clothed while surrounded by bare skin made them stand out, that their clothing was dark from head to toe only compounded it. Each was dressed in their own version of the same, dark jeans, boots, top and jacket.

Willa stepped forward, a wide welcoming smile plastered across her face.

"Hi, Dornan. Aine. How're the plants? My goodness, the girls are... umm. I bet they're into all sorts of mischief."

She knew she was babbling. Willa could feel her face growing hotter under the curious gaze of the four supermodels but she just couldn't help it. The smell that assaulted her the moment she'd approached, was winding its way through her lungs and into her brain, erasing her ability to control her mouth.

"Um, I mean - hi. Welcome... So, umm, what brings you to the mountain?" Willa stammered, trying to focus on forming a coherent sentence.

Four sets of dark ruby eyes met hers as a chuckle ran through the group. Standing slightly off to the side, a distance barely perceptible to the eye but a definite separation by the feel of the groups magic, the tall, dazzling raven-haired beauty was completely still. And when a vampire was still, they really were still. Not a twitch. Not a flicker of an eye lid, not even the slight rise and fall of breath. Absolute immobility. This dark beauty had a slight creased frown marring her exquisite face.

"Thank you. We are happy to be able to join you tonight. Our family only moved here a few weeks ago and we've been looking forward to meeting the community. I am Klaus and this is my family. Daniel, Hayden and Saskia."

Each smiled and greeted Willa and Ella in turn, though when Klaus indicated to the dark-haired beauty her smile faltered as a pained look crossed her face and she caught her plump bottom lip with her sharp fangs, drawing a tiny drop of blood.

Willa's head spun suddenly, conversation became merely white noise, irritating her ears and confusing her already disturbed mind. She could feel her magic rising, uncontrolled, pushing to be set free. If she could tear her gaze from the glittering ruby eyes that were fixed on her, she wouldn't have been surprised to see sparks of magic flowing from her fingers. She had never felt such a lack of control before, even as a new witch learning to master her power she had always felt a strong connection with her magic. A connection that had moved, grown and withdrawn at her will, giving her a level of self-control and influence over her gifts that was the envy of her friends. Panic rose as she tried and failed to catch her grandmothers' attention. Ella was already deep in conversation with the other three vampires. Running her eyes over the group Willa took a small step back, and then another. Tripping slightly over her own feet in the process, caught in the gaze of the silent, motionless vampire. The blood-red eyes flared in the firelight, sending a sharp zing of power through Willa straight to her girly bits. She couldn't stifle the slight moan that accompanied the warm throb between her legs. A moan that reached the sensitive vampire ears and brought a sharp inhalation through the pointed teeth still clamped down on red lips.

What the hell was happening to her? Power threatened to overwhelm Willa as a heat she'd never experienced before rose within her. Her mind whirled with a kaleidoscope of bizarre visuals. Herself wrapped in the arms of the raven vampire. Porcelain pale skin, smooth as polished marble under her fingertips, so real she could almost feel it. A dark garnet drop of blood on a tongue; Hers? The vampires? It didn't seem to matter, the visual alone kicked her heart to a pounding gallop and her eyes almost rolled back in her head with absolute desire. She wanted that blood. She wanted that tongue. She just wanted. She'd never wanted before.

Despite her age, despite the free nature of her Wiccan upbringing, despite the obligatory 'experimental' period that everyone partakes in their adolescence at some stage. She'd never wanted anyone or anything as much as she did right now. Sure she'd had lukewarm, uninspired sex with perfectly average men, but she'd never actually felt desire for her partners. That was just how it was for women, right? Men wanted sex, they desired someone, their bodies responded. Women didn't need to feel desire or attraction in order to participate. It would be a bonus, sure, but it wasn't actually necessary. That's just how it was for Willa. At times in her life, she'd wondered if she were faulty, broken in some fundamental way; she'd even turned her gaze to the abundance of attractive women she saw on campus but they inspired no more reaction than the men. She just wasn't physically or sexually attracted to anyone and for the most part, she was ok with that.

Then this dark angel appeared on her mountain and every hormone her body contained came to life like a bolt of lightning, sending pulsing electrical desire through each microscopic cell. She wanted this woman, more than anything or anyone ever wanted before. She wanted her more than breath, more than life. Her body craved the vampires' touch. Her mind swam with the need to share her every thought and her magic rose uncontrolled, desperately reaching out to the ancient magic of the beautiful creature standing only a few steps away.

As Willa's feet caught on themselves, she pitched backward while her head still spun, not registering her fall. Faster than the gravity that worked against her, a hand the colour of moonlight shot out, reversing her downward direction.

"Are you ok?" A soft, musical voice that would put a sirens song to shame queried. "You kind of went a bit pale and spacey there…"

The hands holding her in place were so delicate and unexpectedly soft, considering the indestructible nature of a vampire. Willa inhaled deeply, the scent of flowers, herbs, of donuts, of moonlight and rain and wind in the trees, filled her lungs to capacity and refused to be released. Her body took in the scent and decided to keep it for her own, not to be exhaled and shared with the universe. Darkness tunnelled her vision until all she could see were sparkling red jewels tinged with concern.

She couldn't talk, Willa's body absolutely rejected the notion.

"I... I..." Willa swallowed against the plug in her throat holding the deliciously scented air inside. "I just..."

And suddenly the raven goddess disappeared from Willa's sight, replaced by absolute darkness. No silver moon, no sparkling stars and tragically no vampire beauty.

Saskia flinched as Willa's eyes rolled upwards into her skull and she collapsed into her arms. Scooping Willa's limp body into her arms, Saskia cradled the small body to her chest. If her heart were still capable of beating, she was sure it would have skipped one or two in the last few minutes. The tiny woman had gone from open and friendly to mute and fighting to breathe in moments. Her sparkling green eyes hadn't shifted from Saskia's face from the moment Willa had approached the vampire family. Saskia had heard Willa's heart race, pumping the sweetest smelling blood to every tiny capillary barely beneath her skin, calling to Saskia, tempting her with its warm, deliciousness. Saskia clamped her teeth tight, rather bite and draw her own blood than give in to the sudden, overwhelming desire to gather this purple-haired angel into her arms, find a dark spot away from the fire, pin her to a tree and sink her aching teeth into the soft skin that was flushed with the greatest meal ever created. For over a hundred years, blood was just blood. Something to sustain her, as necessary to her as food was to humans but if the dim memory of her human life was correct, a lifetime diet of blood was about as desirable as a bowl of porridge. Nutritional but uninspired. However, Willa's blood… It positively called to her. The pink tinge it brought to the witches pale skin, the mouth-watering aroma, Saskia fought against the staggering desire to partake.

And then the angel crumpled into her arms and suddenly Saskia knew that she would never be the same. Her lifeless heart swelled, filled by the woman she cradled. Her first life had ended before she had even had a chance to find love. Her second had brought her the love of her vampire family but never had her mind and magic been overtaken in the same way she'd witnessed in other beings as they found their mates. Gazing down at the entrancing face, so pale and peaceful, Saskia knew in that moment - this was the moment her third life began. A life dedicated to her Wiccan angel, who even without consciousness, turned and inhaled deeply a slight smile playing her lips. The overwhelming aroma was more tempting than ever, pouring from the limp body and yet, when moments ago all she could think of was drinking deeply of Willa's essence, now Saskia wanted nothing less. She would never risk losing herself to her darker nature and in the process risk hurting the amazing creature that the universe had gifted her.

She had no idea if Willa was single. Saskia couldn't smell a mate on her skin but that didn't mean this angel didn't have a human, it only made sense... I mean look at her! Single or taken. It made no difference to Saskia, this woman was hers. Hers to love. Hers to protect. Hers to ensure every happiness and not a moment of the darkness in the world touched. Whether Willa and she would bond as mates or not was irrelevant, Saskia's life from this moment would be forever pledged to this woman.

CHAPTER 2

Willa ran a hand through her hair, flipping it off her shoulder as she carefully avoided Ella's gaze. She'd been peppered Willa with questions for the past hour, refusing to accept Willa's increasingly exasperated 'I don't know' as an appropriate answer. Supposedly, she should know exactly what had happened the previous night.

What? Why? How? All questions that had been plaguing her since the gentle itch of foreign magic had irritated her enough to open her eyes. Being greeted by the two gleeful, giggling faces of Dornan and Aine's young daughters Rhiannon and Neela, who were attempting to concentrate their magic and 'heal' her if the giggled conversation was to be believed. Willa wasn't exactly sure that she even needed healing but if she did the junior Fae magic was only causing an uncomfortable irritation rather than any sort of relief. Willa was surprised to find herself laid out atop a soft, moss-covered log, tucked into a shadowed corner away from the firelight where the full moon party continued uninterrupted. It was like she'd been flipping the tv channels, one moment she was arriving at the party, looking forward to mingling and spending the night stepping out of her responsible 'human' life and indulging in magic with her community. The next thing she knew, her head was spinning like a top while her heart raced and then she was here - lying on a log being magically experimented on by two pint-sized fairies.

According to Ella, she'd fainted straight into the arms of a very flustered vampire. Vampires don't get flustered... Do they? Willa didn't remember any vampires ever living on the mountain. The fact that she had no memory of meeting the coven of newcomers was hugely disappointing. She couldn't believe her bad luck. Apparently, they'd been very warm (the pun had been lost on Ella when Willa had giggled) and personable for the most part. A quartet of mates, each exceptionally stunning, who had heard about the supernatural community on the mountain and decided that a life with less hiding from humans was tempting. It was amazing how much information Ella had managed to gather in such a short amount of time.

But back to the issue at hand – Willa had fainted like a complete idiot and missed out. That was driving her even more crazy than Ella's constant questions as to why she'd taken a dive in the first place. How the heck was she supposed to know why? She was a witch, not the doctor her parents wanted her to be, and despite her vast knowledge of chemistry, biology and how to work the two in harmony for health benefits, actually diagnosing things was absolutely NOT within her scope. All Willa wanted to do today was take a nap, followed by a herbal bath to cleanse her aura for the week ahead. The fact that she felt fine now just fuelled Ella's fire and made Willa want to put the whole experience into the 'ignore it' file. If she left now, and traffic wasn't too bad, she might have enough time to cook up a new batch of skin cream – maybe something with fresh lavender or a touch of lily pilly oil, something soothing to use at the end of a stressful day. There was nothing better than throwing on her pyjamas and slathering herself in cool creams that detoxed all the chemicals of the day while nourishing her parched skin.

Sighing wistfully, Willa dismissed her daily dream of giving 'it' all up and just spending her days creating potions and lotions that made a girl look and feel good, rather than trying to cure cancer. Ella would be all for her giving up the city girl life, chucking in her job at the 'soul-sucking corporation that wants everyone on a pill for everything', and to live the hippie life with her here in the mountains. Ella would potter about all day doing whatever it was she did and talking Willa's ear off on the medicinal potential of whatever new plant the Fae were propagating in their nursery... It would be a dream come true, but Willa could never admit that out loud. Not without risking the wrath and eternal disappointment of her parents who already felt she spent far too much time on the mountain. No, that dream would stay locked deep down inside her, she'd continue to play the dutiful daughter, the responsible scientist and keep her dreams to her own little kitchen.

"Ella, I really, truly don't know why I passed out. But since I'm fine today I don't think we need to worry too much about it. And as for the vampires, well if they're here to stay I'm sure I'll meet them again another time – I'll be back for next full moon party, maybe then."

The slight uptick in her heart caused butterflies to take off in her stomach at the mere mention of the vampires, was distracting as Willa scooped up her keys and dropped a kiss on Ella's cheek.

"I'm off, I still have some stuff to get done at home before work, better to head out now, Sunday traffic and all."

Holding her watch up indicating the time, Willa couldn't help but wonder, what time did vampires wake up, or rise, or whatever? The sudden visual of deep ruby eyes and matching lips drifted through her mind, along with a deep, stomach clenching desire.

Ella placed a hand gently on Willa's cheek, smiling slightly in a way Willa had never seen her do before. The old girl was up to something, that much she could tell, but whatever it was, it could wait. If Willa quizzed her now she knew Ella would talk, at great length about whatever was prompting that look.

Turning her car down the winding mountain road, Willa gave a distracted wave to the two mini fairies she spotted weaving jasmine into each others hair as she passed the nursery. Seeing the little ones tickled her mind, almost like it was trying to remember something but couldn't quite settle on a thought. Merging onto the freeway, her nose suddenly filled with the most delicious scent and

Willa desperately wanted to taste whatever smelt that yummy even though her car had a distinct lack of food and was flying along the centre lane heading towards the city.

Note to self, add fainting and olfactory hallucinations to her list of oddities.

Saskia stretched her arms and legs out their full length, tensing her muscles and then relaxing as she shifted on the chaise she'd claimed as her own. Another day almost done, one of the hundreds, thousands, she'd seen in her time. You'd think that they would all kind of blur together eventually, and you'd be right. Until today that was. Today was the first day of forever. The first day of the rest of her life, her new life… Well her new, new life when she thought about it. And that's what she'd spent all day doing – thinking about it. About her. About them.

Having the lavender haired beauty collapse in her arms last night had been something totally unexpected in a lifetime of routine, boring vampire existence. There was not a lot that was classed as unexpected in her life these days, but that went directly to the top of the list. Only to be knocked down a few spots by the intense longing she felt gazing at the unconscious woman and the almost overwhelming desire to feast upon her. She smelled so sweet, like a fine wine saved for extra special occasions. The steady, if somewhat fast, beat of her heart filled Saskia until she was almost fooled into thinking it was her own, if not for the slight pulsing of blood through the jugular vein that was so very, very tempting. The sight, the smell, the sound, the feelings she'd never felt in either of her lives. It was all too much. In an instant, she'd practically thrown the poor girl at the Fae couple her coven was chatting with, and then she'd bolted. Full out vamp speed, away from the clearing, away from the party, away from the temptation of 'just a taste' that she had a feeling would end in her getting 'shitfaced'. Like a total drunk, she knew that something that smelled that good would taste even better and there is no way she'd be able to stop herself – She'd drink her fill. She'd drink her dry. And that thought would turn her stomach if she were still alive.

And so she ran back home. To where it was safe. To where she could sit and obsess. The spinning thoughts were still egged on by the lingering scent of the woman that clung to her clothes. Sure she could have showered, changed immediately, or at some stage in the last 18 hours. The fragrance tortured her, bringing kinds of desires to mind that at best were impossible and at worst deathly dangerous and yet, there were moments when she inhaled deeply and let her mind become wrapped in the smell, she felt a sense of peace, warmth, and utter contentment that she'd never felt before. And she knew that the woman was the cause. The young witch was simultaneously her greatest desire and her worse. Her ultimate daydream and nightmare.

Days were long when you're a vampire. There is only so much you can do to fill the daylight hours when you're stuck inside while the world and life are happening without you. She'd tried to sleep – yes vampires sleep. They don't need to, what with the whole being dead thing, she never actually got tired, but her body remembered how and it was usually a good way to kill some daylight hours. Saskia had tossed and turned in her bed for what felt like an eternity (but it turns out was only just under 2 hours). Every time she'd closed her eyes to sleep, all she could see was Willa. Her smile as she approached their group. Her peaceful face as she lay in Saskia's arms.

And so what did she do all day? Saskia gave into temptation and daydreamed about Willa. She wanted to find Willa, to know her. She wanted to talk, laugh and spend hours and hours of conversation sharing experiences and lives with her. What sort of life could they have if she were human? And this only fuelled Saskia's favourite pastime, fantasizing about a life of what-ifs. Was she single or already taken? Some nice human boyfriend or worse still a husband? Maybe not, she arrived at the party with her grandmother, not with a date. Maybe she was single. Maybe, she was gay. Could Willa and she be together if she weren't a vampire? Would they live on the mountain, or somewhere else? What did Willa do all day? Was she a sun lover or did she prefer to stay indoors? Did she enjoy summer with trips to the beach and long hot days? Or was she a winter girl, snuggling in woolly jumpers in front of an open fire as the rain pelted down outside? Was she an early riser? Did she sit and watch the sunrise as she began her day or did she fall out of bed at the last possible moment? Half asleep as she ran off to some job with a coffee in hand.

Sometime in the late afternoon, Saskia had drifted from the pitch darkness of her bedroom out to the 'sunroom'. The house was quiet, but then it usually was at this time of day. The others would be off in their rooms, working, napping, reading, indulging in one of the plethoras of hobbies they all had to stave off the boredom of daytime when you lead a nocturnal lifestyle. But this room was generally where they knew they could find Saskia. They knew she still struggled with their life, even after all this time. It's why they'd built the sunroom in the first place. When Klaus had designed the house he hadn't explained the significance of the feature wall, and to be honest, Saskia hadn't been particularly interested in the intricacies of design. Her only requests had been an ensuite bathroom big enough for a jumbo-sized sunken tub – a girl needs a jumbo bubble bath to soak in, right? And a kitchen big enough to cook whatever she wanted… Oh, and free reign to order whatever appliances she wanted for her kitchen. What could she say, everyone had their little secrets and hers was that if she had her way, she'd be the Martha Stewart of the vampire world.

But the sunroom, well, that had been a complete surprise. By the drawn plans she'd assumed it was just a run of the mill family room, and it was technically. But it was Saskia's room really, just as the chaise she'd spent the afternoon curled up on belonged to everyone, but the family understood it was hers from the moment the furniture deliverers had unloaded it. Klaus had taken one look at how Saskia's face had lit up with amazement and delight as he single-handedly hefted the long solid chair across the room and angled it just so - slightly to the side and back from the floor to ceiling wall of smokey UV blocking glass that looked out over the valley, creating a front-row seat to the most spectacular sunsets. From that very first sunset Saskia had known that no matter what happened, she'd never leave this place. Even when the rest moved on, as they must at some stage, she'd stay here forever, in the home that Klaus had tunnelled into the side of the mountain, safe from the daylight and yet able to provide Saskia with a glimpse of what she missed the most from her old life. The sun.

Oh, how she missed the sun. She used to love to just sit outside, her face raised like a sunflower, feeling the heat on her skin, the bright light glowing through her closed eye lids. When she'd been human she and her mother had quarrelled about it almost daily. It wasn't done to sit and soak up the sun. Pale, porcelain skin was the mark of a cultured lady, only the lower classes were tanned and wrinkled from sun exposure. And ultimately, her love of sunshine had led to her life's end. And had teased her ever since – until Klaus had gifted her the sunset again. Even if it was muted through the treated glass, even if she couldn't feel it warm her skin, it was still sunlight.

Was Willa watching the sunset? Was she in a car somewhere, trying to block the glare of light from her vision as she drove? Was she lying outside under a tree listening to the birds find their perches for the night as the sky glowed golden and cast long shadows? Or was she inside a climate-controlled building, completely oblivious to the spectacular light show that nature provided?

Soon the sun would completely dip below the horizon completely, ending yet another day and freeing Saskia to the night. The family would be working tonight but not Saskia. Standing she reluctantly turned her back on the gathering dusk and strode purposefully towards Hayden's study. She could hear the keyboard even through the solid timber door, the same notes had been playing over and over for hours, each time slightly differing in tempo or key. Daniel and Hayden had been working on the same song for days, it sounded great to Saskia but apparently it 'wasn't quite right' – according to Daniel anyway.

Poking her head around the door Saskia smiled at the scene that greeted her. Daniel and Hayden were both seated before the keys. Daniels long legs spread to make room for his beloved to nestle on the stool between them as all four hands plucked and teased the tune from the keys. Daniel's eyes were closed as he nuzzled Hayden's hair singing words in a whisper that would be inaudible to humans. Hayden smiled, her hands pausing on the keys at Saskias appearance.

"I'm going to skip work tonight, got stuff to do in town…" Saskia murmured, hating to disturb them.

Hayden's eyes sparkled as she giggled, "I kinda figured. Good luck babe."

Shaking her head Saskia withdrew. Good luck? Good luck with what? She was just going into the city, not curing cancer. When Hayden and Daniel got into composing they lost all sense of reality and everything became all lovey-dovey, pink hearts and fairytales. All she was doing was seeing if she could find where Willa lived, maybe catch a glimpse if she were extremely lucky.

Ok, so maybe she'd take Hayden's good luck after all.

CHAPTER 3

Ok, so she was officially losing her ever-loving mind, Willa decided as she let her apartment door slam shut behind her and threw her bag into the general direction of the hall stand.

Sure, it wasn't exactly midday bright sunshine outside, but it was still daylight… Well, twilight anyway. So having her head on a constant swivel and almost dislocating her shoulder hanging halfway out of a tram while attempting to catch a glimpse of the tall, figure with long jet hair she'd spotted as the tram passed an alleyway in the city, well it was just ridiculous. There was no way any vampire was traipsing about the early evening in the middle of knock off time in the city, let alone her vampire.

Her vampire? So that was a weird thought. She didn't know the vampires from the full moon party, let alone have a vampire she'd kind of like to maybe call her own. Sure she fully intended to attend again next month and remedy the whole meeting situation, but as for 'her vampire'? Well, why was her brain conjuring that thought when she didn't even remember what they looked like, let alone if she was attracted to any of them? Sure, she knew from Ella that they were a quartet, 2 male, 2 female, and the whole matching pairs thing seemed to speak of 'no luck for you Willa', even if she were attracted to one. So realistically, being on a constant lookout for a vampire whenever she set foot outside her lab, in broad daylight, was just her imagination getting the best of her. She'd never thought of herself as hard up or desperate to meet 'the one' but the past 48 hours of daydreams, what if's and bizarre hormonal cravings made her think she was definitely in need of getting laid.

Right! It was Monday night and there was no way she could spend the whole week, let alone the next month checking every dark doorway and shadowed alley she passed in the hope of not only spotting a vampire, but spotting the vampire that she had no recollection of, in the hope that her body just somehow magically recognized it. And then what? She'd break into song while small birds dropped flowers from the sky, or she was swept off her feet and into a set of iron-strong arms while needle-sharp teeth did unspeakable and life-changing and possibly ending, things to her neck... Wow was it suddenly hot in here?

No, she needed a plan. Tonight, she'd hit up a few of her more discreet 'supe' friends. She knew the vampires' names. Who knew, maybe she'd find them? Maybe there would be photos and she'd immediately recognize whichever vampire her brain seemed to have fixated on. Wait, did vampires photograph? Or was it like mirrors and the whole no reflection thing? Something else to add to her 'odd thoughts' list. She should search vampire hangouts too. Who knows, maybe her local pub held a secret 2 for 1 vampire entry deal on ladies night or something. I mean, they had to get their blood somewhere, and since she hadn't noticed any blood bank burglaries on the news recently it was a fair guess that they fed on people around the city somewhere. But then maybe it wasn't as boring as that. Maybe vampires were like in the books she read – all kinky and into the local BDSM scene. Wasn't blood play a real thing? It sure sounded like it, the way some authors wrote it. Ok, so add local BDSM clubs to the search list. And while she was at it, she may as well cover the most obvious bases and buy tickets to Dracula's Restaurant for next weekend too. It seemed unlikely, but maybe vampires went for the whole 'hide in plain sight' thing and what better place to do that than a vampire-themed restaurant.

Hmm, the list was getting pretty long. It would be so much easier and quicker to just head up the mountain and ask Ella. Or maybe not Ella. She was sure to get all worked up and want to know why she was asking about the vampires, Willa realized. Even if Ella knew where they lived and what they did all day and night, getting that information from her would cost a whole lot more energy and tolerance than Willa was prepared for. Dornan and Aine would probably know, and they wouldn't ask questions if she just happened by the nursery and brought the topic up. However, they'd also likely appraise Ella of any conversation by the time she made it out of their carpark. Ok, tiresome foot search it was.

Pausing at the sliding glass door leading from the living room onto her tiny balcony, Willa's eyes searched the gathering darkness. There were still so many people moving up and down the footpath illuminated more by passing cars with bright headlights than the weak glow from streetlights. She could barely tell male from female in this light, there was tall shadows and short, thin and chunky but none made her heart race or her breath catch in her throat the way the mere thought of the vampire she couldn't recognize did. Was it out there? Did it have daydreams about her? Snorting as the thought, Willa yanked the blinds closed.

Rolling her eyes to herself, she grabbed the phone book and flipped to Michaels. She couldn't believe she was doing this, it was utterly hair-brained but since it seemed her mind wasn't about to move onto another topic any time soon... Well, she may as well chase this and see where it led. If nothing else, at least she'd learn a bit about vampires in the process...

Sending a quick prayer to the great goddess as she searched. There were so many. Which Michaels were they? The V Michaels in Boronia? V for Vampire? Or perhaps the K Michaels in Ferntree Gully? Both were close enough to the mountain community that they were possible... As were the 247 other Michaels's in the northeastern suburbs? And who knew, did vampires have telephones? Did they like to call each other and shoot the breeze during the daylight hours when they were confined to their homes? Or did they spend those hours in their coffins like in the movies, and therefore had no need for a telephone? Her breath caught in her chest as the dark jewelled eyes floated behind her lids. Teasing her, calling to her, drawing her entire focus until she gave up searching through hundreds of random Michaels phone numbers.

Ok, so humans were confusing. You'd think after all these years living amongst them, studying them, and before that, actually being a human, would make finding one single witch easier. But not so. The little witch was amazingly absent from anywhere she should be. Saskia cast her eyes to the east, where the sky was just beginning to lighten. The sun would be up soon and she'd spend another day trapped inside her home while the need to stride through the streets of the city to find the Wiccan who had planted herself firmly in her daydreams, drove her slowly insane. It'd be another day wasted. Why couldn't she just be where she should be? Ok so it was a long, very long time ago, but in her Saskia's day, witches were surprisingly easy to find. They knew their place as did everyone else. And they stuck to it so as to be easily found when needed. She understood that these days very few people practised the old ways of Wicca, witches were more likely just everyday people who had read a few books and preferred the idea of an ancient belief system that wasn't based on the patriarchy of Christianity.

She'd started the week thinking it would be simple. She'd find her purple-haired witch in some local gem shop or Chinese herbalist. She may or may not orchestrate an 'accidental' meeting and they'd get to know each other. That was the idea. The reality was frustratingly different. Monday evening when Saskia had headed into the city she'd weaved in and around the crowds of commuters leaving their offices en masse. She'd ducked in and out of every crystal seller, herbal store and fortune teller in China town without success. She'd spent hours casing out the stacks of the ancient religion section of the massive state library and then began crisscrossing the city popping into any and every old book store and naturopath she found. At one stage she'd thought she was about to strike gold or lavender as was more accurate. She'd been making her way down a filthy, unnamed side alley that ran between other smaller alleys just off the Burke Street mall. There was a hole in the wall store tucked at the end that was owned by a well known gypsy fortune teller. Just the kind of place a witch should frequent. Just as she'd been about to push her way through the 70's style beaded curtain draped over the open doorway, her chest had suddenly tightened. It had only been a few fleeting seconds but she felt as though the air had been knocked out of her lungs. Spinning 360 right there in the threshold, she'd been sure she would find herself eye to eye with her missing Wiccan, only to find... Nothing. A bored-looking middle-aged woman wearing jeans and a t-shirt was dealing tarot cards on a counter in the dim store, the alleyway was empty and from what she could see of the streets at the far end, the usual commuter coming and goings were, well, coming and going. She'd even gone as far as dashing out onto the main thoroughfare just in case, but life was going on as usual without any sight of Willa.

Returning to the fortune teller was a complete waste of precious minutes.

"What you seek – seeks. What you have lost – you will become, until neither the lost nor the found are lost again."

Vague much! What sort of fortune tells talks in vague generalisations and riddles? Saskia fumed. What was the point in paying for guidance unless you could actually have your questions answered?

By Thursday she'd covered every mystical book store in the entire city, either in person for those that stayed open after dark, or by phone during daylight hours. She'd made an appearance at every place of worship no matter the denomination, interrupted a few 'pagan' gatherings that had fliers posted in various incense and candle stores around the city – which evidently were just a bunch of people sitting around drinking herbal tea and discussing television. Not exactly a top-level mystical gathering.

Friday night, she lurked in the shadows of the botanical gardens closely watching arrivals and departures from a large gathering of actual genuine supernatural creatures who lived as humans according to the discreet listing in the classifieds section of the Brunswick News. The group was a large and lively one. Everyone was laughing and chatting freely, but owing to the extremely public venue, there was none of the free-flowing magic and embracing of other forms that she'd witnessed at the mountain gathering. It was all quite 'vanilla' really. Even the fae and the nymphs, while they danced and wore flower crowns they wove for each other – the dancing was more just spinning each other in circles as little children would do, and the crowns, while decorative were all precut, stems directly from the florist to hair. The gathering was more 'mystical lite' than a truly spiritual event. And needless to say, there was not even a glimpse of Willa. By midnight Saskia got bored and spent the rest of the dark hours just wandering aimlessly along the river until she was deep into suburbia.

It was now almost dawn, and by tonight she'd have been searching for a full week for a single witch who just couldn't be found. Maybe that was the basis of her magic, Saskia pondered. Maybe she could appear and disappear at will, maybe she could visit other realms or time travel. Man, she'd be pissed off if Willa had been hanging out in 1870 all week. A whole week, when she could have been working, reading, baking, sewing… Doing any number of other things day or night, but she'd spent every waking moment – which equated to every moment, every blasted, slow-moving minute since Saturday night, searching for a witch she knew nothing about.

Kicking at the dew covered leaves underfoot Saskia walked onto the train platform just as the early morning train squealed into the station. Normally, she preferred to drive when she was out and about, but these past days, she'd been on foot or public transport. So much more sensible than constantly being on the lookout for parking when she could be on the lookout for purple hair. And who knew, maybe Willa would just step onto a train or tram right before her eyes. If she couldn't come up with any more search ideas today, she'd either have to swallow her pride and pay a visit to the nice Fae couple with the nursery on the mountain - they seemed to know Willa, or just get ahold of her self respect and give up.

The tightening band around her still heart told her which situation it preferred, and it wasn't the one that left her with much dignity. Since when does a vampire ask for help with anything? Let alone from a fairy. Slumping onto a grimy seat, Saskia's head swam, spinning and tilting suddenly before righting itself. Closing her eyes to the lightning sky she tried to quiet her mind against a weeks lack of peace, relaxation and most importantly, food. Something had to give. If she didn't eat soon, if or when she found Willa, their interaction might not last past hello. After tonight, she really needed to admit defeat, give up the search and return to real life or risk losing her carefully developed self-control.

Willa's head spun and she stumbled as she squeezed through the closing train doors. An entire night propping up the bar the largest BDSM nightclub in the city had given her a pounding headache, feet that absolutely refused to stand in her heels at this moment and utter exhaustion that she was hard-pressed to fight off. And for what? To stand for hours in a stifling crowd watching them spank, tease and tie each other up? Sure there'd been a few vampires blending into the crowd looking for willing blood kink players. But all she'd gotten by the end of the night was a stomach full of nausea and a disturbed nap on the cross-city train. Hell, the exhaustion had almost taken her over enough that she didn't even recognize her stop until the last moment. Hopping from the train as it jerked to life, her stomach flipped again. Had she drunk anything other than lemonade in the past few hours she'd have embarrassed herself. Watching the carriages dotted with equally weary party goers zip past in the predawn light, Willa concluded that she either needed to call her search quits, or talk to Dornan and Aine. There was no way she could spend another week working all day and vampire hunting all night.

CHAPTER 4

"Who would have known it was so hard to find one single, little, insignificant witch," Saskia grumbled, throwing herself onto her chaise.

Willa had yet again been at the forefront of her mind all day and no matter what she did, what random activity she'd attempted to turn her focus to, her attention refused to be distracted from its obsessive thoughts. She'd almost cracked and searched the phone book. She hated the thought, though quickly remembered that she didn't know Willa's last name. Then she'd cracked a little more and quizzed an amused Daniel and Klaus and a slightly sympathetic Hayden about their interaction with the grandmother. Now not only was she still obsessing over finding Willa but she was fuming to the point that she could almost picture steam coming from her ears like some children's cartoon. An entire day of humiliation and knowing smirks from her family had netted no actual useful information. And certainly nothing concrete as to where she lived or how she could be found.

The sum total of their combined efforts equated to the knowledge that Willa had two parents who appeared for all intents and purposes to be human and highly driven career-wise. She'd attended university gaining a degree in Science from which she'd graduated a few years prior. How can someone be so hard to find in this day and age? Hell, Klaus was 476 years old, with over 90% of his life being lived before the invention of modern technology and even he was listed in the phone book, both personally and in the business pages.

The sun had dropped below the horizon as Saskia sat huffing with frustration, even the kaleidoscope of colours neglected to distract her today.

"You know, there are two solutions to your witch problem…" Hayden perched on the high back of the chaise and gently stroked Saskia's hair. "You have a choice. You can pull out your 'big girl teeth' and head over to the Fae house. They seemed to know her pretty well, they're bound to be able to give you the scoop."

"Or?" Saskia dreaded the answer, she already knew what it was going to be.

"Or - you move on. Go out. Find someone to get a bite to eat from. Put her out of your mind and then get your ass back to work. I know we get by pretty well on a night to night basis, but you haven't been in all week… We kinda need you. Daniel was looking pretty tragic last night."

Saskia couldn't help but roll her eyes and growl dramatically at the suggestion.

"Oh, vamp up!" Hayden giggled. "You're not some kid asking classmates to pass notes to a cute girl. You're a grown woman. More than grown if you take into account the fact that you're probably about 100 years older than her. Go ask where she lives then get your ass over there."

Saskia knew that the solution was simple, but for some reason, she felt like one of those teen girls from movies, asking her crush's friends if they think she'd like her.

"I love you girl, but either way you need to feed. A hungry vampire is a bitch to live with and babe, you're skirting that line pretty closely. So, you can either get some fast food or talk to the Fae and get gourmet... Your choice."

Saskia shuddered as Hayden released the braid she'd been fashioning in Sass's long hair and drifted out the door into the darkened bush, no doubt going in search of a snack of her own. She was hungry. She freely admitted that. But the thought of eating with anyone other than Willa made her stomach turn and yet the thought of dining on her, while such an enticingly delicious thought, was equally stomach-churning. Was there such a thing as a vampire who just didn't eat at all? Could she become vamporexic? She knew of those who existed only on animals, forgoing human blood. But the scent of fur had always made her gag in such a way she could never force it near her mouth let alone drink. Would she be the worlds first completely 'celibate' vampire, existing only on the air she didn't need to breathe? A hungry, raving bitch who would have to live a solitary life locked away from both the human and supernatural worlds due to her malevolent personality.

"Hello Dornan, Aine, I was wondering if you could tell me where the witch Willa who fainted last week and warped my mind, lives?"

Saskia grimaced at her reflection in the glass and she tried the request on for size. No task had ever felt more daunting or uncomfortable and that included her very first days as a vampire when all she'd wanted to do was throw herself into the sunshine and burn while simultaneously drinking anyone who happened by.

Yep, as much as she didn't want to ask the Fae for help. She was going to swallow her pride and do just that.

Willa's knee jumped, dancing a nervous jig as she sat silently under Dornan's gaze. Thank goodness Ella wasn't hanging out at the nursery today. It was no coincidence that today just happened to be the day she made the trip to visit the supes living by the sea three hours away. She'd kept to the same schedule for as long as Willa could remember, two weeks after the full moon, Ella would spend a day and night with her friends on the beach. They'd share the latest gossip from their communities, trade spells and charms, drink copious amounts of sangria from Ella's old barrel esky and drunkenly sing the night away around a fire as the waves licked the sand. Willa remembered the first time Ella had taken her along, she'd been 17 and it had all seemed like a scene from some kind of Disney movie, except with a lot more alcohol and swearing involved.

Knowing Ella's schedule had been the entire reason she was here today. She'd have at least 16 hours before Ella was back and Dornan outed her. And out her, he would. The moment Ella was back she'd hear about Willas visit and then… Well then, there would be no hope of the peace and solitude to either find and get to know Saskia or to sulk and try to put this little obsession behind her. Yes, Willa knew she was on borrowed time, and Dornan sitting there with an amused smile on his face, was wasting precious minutes. That and his silence was making her antsy.

"So… Do you know where I can find them? The vampires? I mean, there's not a whole lot around here that you don't know. Sometimes I think you know even more about what's going on in the community than Ella. But then again, between both of you guys, you seem to be the unofficial census of supes here on the mountain, so I figured if anyone would know about them it would be you… Or her. But you probably already know why I'm here and not asking Gran. I mean, she means well, but oh, she pretty much did my head in with her questions after the full moon party. Can you imagine what she'd be like if I asked her where to find them? Hell, in her mind I'd either be married off or vampire dinner before I even finished speaking. Hey! Don't laugh, you know it's true."

The sight of Dornan's amused smirk brought a quick end to Willa's nervous rambling.

"Aye, right about that, you are young Willa. Your gran would have things to say if she knew of your interest, and say them she would. A whole lot of them. But no matter, say them she still will, just tomorrow and not today." Dornan chuckled.

Willa couldn't help but roll her eyes. She had no idea how old the Fae were, they looked to be about her age but she knew for sure they were much older than they seemed. That they'd known Ella as a child together with their odd turn of speech always seemed to make Willa feel more like a teenager seeking the approval of the cool kids, rather than a fully functional adult in her own right.

"So, aside from being in the clear for now, your visit holds a reason… Do tell, what it be?"

Willa shook her head confused, "I told you Dornan, I just want to get to know them. I mean, I don't remember even meeting them on the full moon and meeting vampires seems kinda cool. So, I figured I'd, you know… Drop by their house or coffin or whatever, and be neighbourly. I doubt they'd like a welcome sponge cake but I'm sure I can find a butcher with blood sausage somewhere."

Even to her ears, the words rang untrue and the smug look on Dornan's face proved that he knew it too.

"Not true missy. Not the answer of your heart. Tell me true or not at all. Tell me true and I'll tell you…"

A carrot had been dangled, a carrot that Willa didn't want to reach for but one that she strained to grasp at all the same.

"I don't know why Dornan. There's just something about them, or there might be. I don't know. As I said, I don't even remember meeting them, but I can't get them out of my mind. I've been stuck in a vampire obsession loop for weeks now and it's driving me nuts. I can't concentrate on anything other than finding them. It's in my head all day at work. I can barely sleep and when I do I dream of vampires. Even stupid things like looking at the sunset when I'm on the tram after work, or when the sky is turning pink in the early morning - I wonder if they're seeing it too. Then I wonder if they ever see the sunrise or set. How long since they have? Do they sleep all day? Do they go out at night? And if they do where?"

Willa couldn't slow the torrent of words that spilled from her, If it meant Dornan would impart his knowledge then she'd tell him anything he wanted to know… Hell, she'd give him her bra size if it helped.

"Not them I think, you're interested in.' He nodded, "Not all but one. The one. Clearly, I see it and see it already does Ella too. See clearly you will soon. Moments take time, but not much, never fear. You have come now because it is time. Whether Ella be here or there is of no consequence. But better there, for now, I think. Better it is only two and not three."

Wow, cryptic much? Again! Willa thought. This was the problem with talking to Fae, they talked in riddles that Yoda would be proud of, you could barely understand a thing they said half the time. The unfurling of Dornan's silver wings drew her from her inner snark just in time to watch him flit above the ferns and disappear into the twilight shadows.

"My littles have your answer, stay a moment, they know the time." His voice floated through the air to Willa, sounding all too pleased with himself.

See, this was why vampires stuck to themselves and didn't generally get involved in the supernatural community. Bloody fairies, with their backwards talk, secrets and smiles. It wasn't enough that Saskia had lowered herself, swallowed her pride along with a large, juicy steak. No, now she was left in the care of these pesky little fireflies. Aine had seemed quite nice at the full moon gathering, warm and chatty enough, but today she just smiled her self satisfied smile, talked about the time like she was a white rabbit late for tea and disappeared just as quickly as one. Leaving Saskia alone with her children who seemed more interested in buzzing about her like mosquitos than anything else. And all without even offering a clue as to where she could find Willa. Damn, bloody irksome Fae. Ask a simple question, and get nothing close to an answer.

The little pests were circling, their small pastel wings beating at a great rate just to keep their feet off the ground. They giggled and sang to each other as they twirled around her. Silly little songs, for silly little girls. I wonder what would happen if I swatted one like a fly? Saskia mused. No, better not. Fae are pretty much undestroyable but these were kids, after all. It wouldn't be the most polite move to give them a vamp strengthened back hand.

The older one was attempted to tug her along. Glancing about, Saskia still couldn't find their mother, damn, if she'd needed a babysitter surely there were better options than a vampire with a craving for a witch. Allowing herself to be towed along the bottom of the gully like a pet, Saskia's mind drifted, time to come up with a plan B, or C or whatever version her search had reached by this stage.

The giggles and singing faded to mere background noise, drowned out by the beating heart that seemed to be growing within her chest. Her mind spun and dipped as the singing duo breached the draped skirt of a weeping cherry tree and the earth suddenly stopped moving altogether.

"Willa and Sassy, under a tree. K. I. S. S. ING!" The giggling fairies sang as they twirled and danced through the hanging branches and disappeared.

Leaving Saskia face to face with a lavender haired witch who looked like she was about to either vomit or smack one of the little Fae herself.

CHAPTER 5

Willa's eyes widened and her stomach lurched. She could barely formulate a coherent thought. The very person she'd been searching out for weeks now, was standing right before her. Surrounded by garlands of blossoming flowers as the tinkling giggles of little fae played in the background. It was like something out of a Disney movie but old Walt never cast a witch or a vampire in the starring role.

"Oh my god... It's you!" she gasped. "Sorry, I know that's kinda stating the obvious, but yep – It's you, kinda sums it up."

A tiny ghost of a smile drifted across the dark goddesses face for a moment and then disappeared back behind the porcelain doll perfection of her blank expression.

"What are you doing here?" Willa cringed, her question came out in a high pitched squeak. Yep way to keep her cool. " I'm here to visit with Aine and Dornon obviously. I've known them most of my life... There's nothing unusual about me visiting my friends. Is there? Umm, I'm Willa by the way. I'm not sure if we were actually introduced the other week. I'm embarrassed to say I don't have much of a memory of that night, which kinda sucks since I wasn't even drunk. I totally had the hangover without any of the fun…"

Willa clamped her teeth together tightly in an effort to stem the random babble spilling from her mouth. Glancing up she was met with glittering ruby eyes and her attempts at controlling her tongue cracked.

"Sorry, I bet I sound like a complete idiot and I promise I'm not. I just can't seem to shut up right now."

Pulling in a lung full of air Willa tried to control all the thoughts tumbling through her mind. It didn't help. Suddenly every fibre of her being zinged to life. She could feel her magic sparking through her veins. She didn't know what she expected a vampire to smell like – death or blood maybe? But this vampire. WOW! She smelled like sunshine and wattle and cinnamon and old books with just a tiny hint of something that reminded Willa of the snow that occasionally fell on the mountain mid-winter. There was no way that spending time with Saskia was going to ease her obsession, just one sniff of the air had Willa's mind focusing even closer.

And through all the swirling thoughts and spinning senses that Willa was battling in those moments, Saskia was a statue, standing tall and oh so still. Not a flicker of anything – not a thought, not an emotion, not the slightest reaction showed on her face.

"Umm, so anyhoo… Yeah. Are you going to say anything or should I just keep babbling?"

She giggled uncomfortably under Saskia's intense gaze. This was not how she'd seen this meeting going. A slight movement caught her attention, the slim column of the vampire's neck moved slightly, as though she was swallowing a lump similar to the one Willa felt in her own throat.

Saskia's brows pulled together in a slightly pained expression and two long, sharp fangs appeared as she opened her mouth to speak.

"Shhorry. I… I shhore thish going differently."

Her voice was low and slightly throaty as Saskia spoke, reminiscent of a nightclub blues singer Willa thought. The sort of voice she could close her eyes and listen to for hours and still be happy.

"Pleash, jusht give me a minute. I need… I jusht need to…"

Saskia's hands fisted at her sides and she closed her eyes, drawing in unnecessary deep breaths as though needing to steady herself in the same way Willa did.

Saskia dropped her head and opened her eyes, staring fixedly at her shoes.

"I'm sho shorry. Thish hash never happened to me before. I mean, I've shmelt lotsh of people who shmell pretty good but it'sh never been like thish. My fangsh only appear when I want them to. But you shmell sho damn good, it'sh like I can't control them… I promish not to eat you though. I really want to but I promish not to. You can trusht me."

Willa stood stunned, turning Saskia's strange words over in her mind. A small amused smile tugged at her lips even as she fought to hide it.

"Are you saying that your fangs aren't out all the time? Sorry for asking, but I don't know a whole lot about vampires. You guys are kinda into keeping secrets, even from other supes."

Saskia hung her head again, shame overwhelming her.

"Yesh."

"And they popped out because I smell good? Like without you meaning for them to?"

Willa had given up trying to control her face and was losing the battle with the giggle she could feel pushing to be let free. As free as Saskia's fangs.

"Yesh. I've never shmelt anything or anyone like you before… It'sh amayshing. Like if heaven were a shmell and you rolled around in it and then you were sherved up as my lasht meal before I die..."

That did it, there was just no holding back when a goddess like Saskia said you smelled like heaven while her fangs glistened long and beautiful, and strangely tempting. Willa so wanted to run the tip of a finger over them.

"Oh. My. God. Saskia, you totally have a lady vampire boner for me, don't you?"

And with that the laughter Willa had been holding down with every ounce of her self control broke to the surface.

Saskia rolled her eyes and sighed. Over a hundred years of afterlife and this was the first time ever she'd felt an emotion she remembered from her human life – complete and utter embarrassment. Willa was right, she was like a teenage boy with a hard-on for the pretty girl.

Crossing her legs she sagged gracefully to the ground, keeping her gaze on the blades on grass before her.

"Ok shure, laugh it up. Thish ish shtoopid. Yesh, you smell like a wet dream, ok? Like everything anyone, ever fantashished about come to life. I can't help it, sho pleash don't teash."

Willa joined Saskia on the ground, her cross-legged position mirroring Saskia's. Saskia's fangs throbbed with need at Willa's proximity.

"I won't tease anymore Sass, I promish…" Willa lisped with a final chuckle.

"They're so beautiful, so long and white. They look like marble, like the smoothest polished stone I've ever seen. Can I touch one?" Willa's hand reached out tentatively a single index finger extended.

Catching her wrist, Saskia's grip was soft while simultaneously as strong as an iron manacle. Gently returning Willa's hand to her lap Saskia's lips quirked in a half-smile.

"Better not. I know I shaid you can trusht me not to eat you, but maybe you shouldn't put temptation literally in my mouth jusht yet… Like I shaid, I'm not exactly in control of my fangsh right now."

Dear god, Saskia wanted to feel Willa's touch on her fang, or any other part of her she cared to lay hands on.

Willa sat quietly willing herself not to crawl across the ground and into the vampire's lap. She had no idea what was happening to her or why, but she was struggling to control herself just as much as Saskia apparently was. All she wanted to do was get as close to her as possible, and if that put her life at risk as Saskia warned… Well so be it. It'd absolutely be worth dying if she went with the scent of this woman fogging her mind.

Silence descended. Saskia locked down every muscle and fibre of her body. The strong, quick thud thud of Willa's heart echoed through her head and straight to her fangs, parching her throat and tormenting her. Never before had she needed to fight so hard to keep control of herself. She wanted Willa. She wanted to bite her, sure, but she also wanted to simply draw her close and wrap her arms around her. She wanted to stay up all day and night talking, sharing their lives, their hopes, their dreams. She wanted the soft look that Klaus always got when he watched Hayden from across the room. She wanted the hard, hungry look that Daniel wore anytime he watched his mates express their love, moments before his own love flared into a full-blown bushfire of desire. She wanted to be dragged panting and breathless into her bedroom, not to emerge for hours, days. She wanted to giggle, bake cakes, to blow out birthday candles and wrap Christmas presents... She wanted what had been missing first from her life and now her afterlife. She wanted eternity with Willa. It was a heady concept, made more so by the overwhelming aroma of her blood.

Who knew how long they sat, eyes focused on each other, both unconsciously swaying closer only to regain control and back away a little. Almost a seductive dance, each was tentatively taking the first steps.

Drawing a shaky breath, Willa's chest tightened desperate to keep the air that tasted of Saskia.

"I... I'm Willa." She stammered. "I know this is going to sound weird, I mean I don't even get it myself; but I've been looking for you for weeks. And that's not even the weird thing. See the thing is, I have no idea who you are. I mean, I know that we met, but I don't remember. When I passed out, somehow you were completely erased from my memory."

Grimacing, Willa tried not to allow her gaze to be drawn to those pouting, ruby lips, the sliver of pink tongue that ran over them, caressing the ivory fangs that appeared to be receding just a little.

"But there was something left in here." She struggled to form a coherent explanation as she tapped her temple. "I knew that I had to find you for some reason. That's what's so weird… I have no memory of you. No idea what you looked like. What you do. Where you live. But I've spent every night the past few weeks searching for you all over the city… Why? I don't understand."

Saskia swallowed. For a dead person, her mouth was drowning in saliva and the breaths she had no physical need for seemed to constrict her chest. As the witches words broke through to her foggy brain her bloody jewelled eyes flared. Could it truly be? Had Willa been running herself ragged searching for her, while she had been starving and doing the same? It's not like Melbourne were New York… Sure it was a city, but it really shouldn't have been so hard for a worldly vampire and a purple-haired young witch to find each other. But then again, if Willa really had no memory of her – well there was some pretty unusual, and powerful magic at play.

"You… You searched for me? How is it possible? I mean, I believe, you… But, I have been searching for you. And I knew what you looked like too."

Saskia leaned forward slightly, practically imperceptible to the human eye but that fraction was the first tiny crack in her marble surface. The second came a heartbeat later as her eyes fell on a minuscule sliver of pale, barely pink skin that marred the perfect alabaster of Willa's hand that was plucking at the grass. Without Saskia even realizing it, a single finger tip ghosted the pink trail as she continued.

"I guess that would be kind of weird for you. Not knowing who I was or what I even look like but feeling driven to find me. It wasn't just you though, so we can be weird together. I've spent every night since the full moon looking for you and I have absolutely no idea why, other than there's just something about you that made me want to know more. To be close to you. You know? And by the way, you're not exactly easy to find yourself. Who would have thought finding a witch with purple hair would be so difficult. Hayden practically force-fed me a rabbit today and kicked me out of the house. I'm not welcome back until I vamped up and asked the Fae for information on how to find you. If I'd known that swallowing my pride would equate to finding you under a tree, I'd have done it weeks ago."

Willa threw back her head and laughed, the sound like a song in Saskia's ears.

"So we're in agreement then... We're both idiots who could have avoided a fair bit of insanity by simply asking for help. You were avoiding your pride and I was just avoiding my granny. She'd get one hell of a kick outta this. But that leads me to my next question. What is this? Exactly. I mean, I'm not exactly an ancient, worldly vampire but I've been around the block often enough to know that there's something different about you... Not that I'm a slut or anything. I mean, you know, I've dated and all, but there's something different about you. And me. Us. Is it a vampire thing? Did you do a whole vampire, compulsion, whammy thing on me that backfired? That would explain the missing full moon party and you thing, as well as my obsession with finding you. Maybe my brain is trying to get itself fixed? Do you think?"

A slight smile tugged the corner of Saskia's mouth as giggles filtered through the curtain of branches.

"Vampire whammy, vampy whampy, vampy whampy..." The singing of two little Fae spies alerted the pair to the fact that they were no longer alone.

"No vampy whampy, I promise," Saskia reassured, rising gracefully to her feet. "If I was going to use compulsion on you trust me, it wouldn't be to erase myself from your memory. Hell, I would have stamped my entire life story on your brain permanently along with my address, if I had the chance. And since we're on the subject, and seem to be entertaining the locals, how about I show you my home right now? Then we can talk without the audience."

Willa nodded, her face lighting up as Saskia gently grasped her hands and brought her to her feet as easily as lifting a feather.

Stepping through the trailing branches, Willa murmured a few words under her breath that meant nothing to Saskia. The squeals of joy and excited giggles that followed as they made their way across the nursery drew a glance over her shoulder in time to see pink and purple blooms magically bursting to life, showering the little fairies with petals as they danced with delight beneath the twilight sky of matching shades.

With a wink, Willa chuckled. "Distraction for a quick getaway."

Linking her pinky finger with Saskia's, Willa lead the way to her beat-up Datsun parked in the empty roadside carpark beside the nursery.

Gingerly climbing into the passenger seat Saskia had her window down at vamp speed.

"Do me a favour? I'm barely holding on, you smell so darn edible. I'm going to need the windows open if we're BOTH going to make it home…"

Willa swallowed the dry lump in her throat and cranked her window fully open.

"I'm not a bite on the first date kinda girl," she whispered with a slight smirk.

CHAPTER 6

The sky slowly morphed from jet to navy, clear and dotted with silver stars visible between the tree tops. Saskia felt a little guilty as she watched Willa's eyes blink rapidly, tearing slightly as her nostrils flared and she fought to hide the yawn. She'd forgotten that most people needed a good nights sleep in order to function. It had been forever since she'd needed to sleep, sure she still did it most days just to stave off the boredom and kill some daylight hours but she didn't actually need to sleep. Not since her new life had begun. She never felt tired, never felt that overwhelming desire to just disappear into the oblivion of restful slumber, never fought to keep her body going. Since she'd become a vampire all she'd ever felt physically was strength and vitality... And hunger.

"You're tired." She observed. "We've been talking all night and I'm guessing you didn't spend yesterday in bed napping the day away. I'm sorry. I'm so used to not needing sleep, to always being awake if I choose to be, it didn't occur to me that this wasn't the ideal way for you to spend your evening."

Willa's smile turned to a grimace as another yawn took over. She couldn't even attempt to hide it or be the least bit ladylike this time. It was a full-blown, gaping mouth, tonsil displaying sigh that only notched her exhaustion up further.

"No, I'm fine. It's fine. I'm just a little tired is all. It's all good." She reassured, even as yet another wave of yawns crashed over her.

"I love your view. It must be incredible to watch the sun rise from here." Willa cringed as she registered her faux pas. "I mean, I suppose it would be. If you could, you know, stand in front of a pane of glass and watch the sun rise without the risk of bursting into flames of course… Sorry, I tend to babble when I'm tired."

Saskia chuckled at Willa's attempt to backpedal.

"The sun always peeks out just over there first at this time of year."

Saskia pointed to a small gap in the trees in the distance where the sky was a smidge lighter than directly overhead. To her eyes, the difference was almost like looking at full daylight and midnight but she realized that Willa would just see it as half a shade lighter than the rest of the night sky.

"The hilltop turns a really pale golden colour, almost like its colour has been washed too many times. Then, the sky changes from black to navy and lightens through a really rich, aqua to pale robin egg blue in less than half an hour. Sometimes, there are beams of gold that filter through the trees, like torchlight that's shining down from heaven highlighting the bush. The birds usually start chattering to each other about an hour or two before the day makes its appearance, but as the sun peeks over the hills and wakes the world they let rip with song. Some days it's like they truly are singing to celebrate the new day. This is my favourite time of day… Well now and sunset. I love the colours, the way every day it's a little different. I love the drama of it."

Willa leaned closer to the glass, watching the sky change with new eyes. As the sun breached the horizon her attention shot to Saskia, sitting calmly as a beam of golden light crept across the ground towards the glass window.

"Saskia? The sun…"

Smiling, Saskia tapped gently on the tinted glass and left her palm resting directly beneath the sunbeam.

"UV proof glass" she explained. "When we built the house, Klaus had it specially made. It's why this is my favourite house we've had. It might have taken more than a century but I love being able to watch the day world again. I didn't even realise I missed it until it was given back to me."

Willa watched with amazement as the dawn washed Saskia's face with its muted colours. She didn't even realise she was moving until her hand settled over Saskia's palm against the glass and their fingers intertwined. This was almost becoming an embarrassment, how often through the night had she unconsciously reached out and touched the dark beauty before her. A light touch of fingers. The brush of a hand on a leg or an arm. She'd really had to fight hard more than once when her creeping hands had those plumb, ruby lips in their trajectory.

When Saskia had directed her up the mountain to her home, Willa's stomach had fluttered wildly, like a junior Fae playing around a bomb fire. Saskia's coven, Hayden, Daniel and Klaus had been welcoming and full of knowing grins and elbow nudges as she'd been introduced. Shortly after her arrival, the trio had announced they were going to get dinner on the way to work and they'd see Saskia in the morning. Bidding Willa goodbye they'd disappeared on foot into the darkness faster than she'd have believed possible.

After a quick tour of the main living space, Saskia and Willa had settled comfortably on opposite ends of the chaise by the window and talked. They'd talked about the strange attraction they both felt and what it might mean. They talked about Willa's work at the pharmaceutical company and how she had always dreamt of being a beautician NOT a chemist. Saskia had explained her work in the family business. Willa found it highly amusing and exceptionally clever that the vampires hid in plain sight. Laughing, it never would have occurred to her that when searching out a vampire, she should check the local drag show for a duet of vampire men, masquerading as show tune singing drag queens five nights a week while Hayden played the piano dressed in 1950's biker fashion. After Saskia had proven she couldn't carry a tune in a bucket, forcing Willa to plug her ears against the screeching sound of bats fighting, she'd laughingly elaborated on her position backstage, making costumes, creating makeup looks, teased, sequined hairdo's and being mother to all, vampire and human queens alike.

Willa had opened up about her own family. Her childhood and teenage years spent visiting her Wiccan grandmother, growing and strengthening her powers within the embrace of the supernatural community that thrived on the mountain. The pressure she felt from her parents to achieve academically and professionally above all else. Her growing dissatisfaction with the direction her life was going but her fear of disappointing her parents should she try to make a change. And most importantly and reluctantly, the sorry state of her personal life. Her face had blazed red as she admitted her apathy towards dating, sex and making emotional connections no matter the gender. Inwardly she was horrified as her mouth spewed the details of her few unfulfilling sexual encounters, but she had no way of stopping herself once she started talking. No matter how loudly her mind screamed to shut up, it seemed important to her soul that Saskia know.

In turn, Saskia had shared her vague recollections of her human life. Of how her mother had ambitions for her to be a 'proper lady', decorative and trained to marry well, while she just wanted to be free. She giggled, retelling how many times she misplaced her gloves, burnt her nose sitting in the sun without a hat or parasol and was caught more than once running barefoot on the hills around their home with her stockings and boots tied around her waist. She was scandalous from a young age and had she been present to witness the aftermath of her death. She was sure that being found clothes shredded, her skin torn and bleeding from dozens of bites, would have caused her mother to have vapours and take to her bed for months while her father ensured a plausible cover story fitting to the tragic death of the daughter of the local peerage was shared with those that mattered.

Willa couldn't help the slow tears that traced their way down her face as she pictured Saskia's life and death. Though many, many, years apart, it struck her that both their parents and younger lives were quite similar. Only she had Ella to look out for her and ensure she was safe and watched over by a community. While Saskia had fought to live her own life and had 'died' alone... Or would have if not for Klaus.

The tall, silent vampire who had gently squeezed her hand on introduction and smiled like an indulgent parent as his gaze moved from Willa to Saskia. He had saved Saskia without even a pause to consider otherwise. Saskia explained that she had no memory of her death or rebirth, though Klaus had told the story once she was regained coherence. He'd come across a pack of feral vampires, playing with their food. They'd tossed her limp, body back and forth between them, each taking a bite, a taster so to speak before tossing her away again. Back and forth she went until Klaus happened on the scene. Horrified at what he was witnessing, but not in the position to stop the ferals, he had waited until they grew bored and moved on. Saskia's body had been removed and, as her state of dress and injuries caused the minister to refuse her a burial in sanctified grounds. It was to the doctors garden shed that Klaus had followed her. His keen vampire hearing had picked up the faint, very sporadic, heartbeat when even the doctor declared her life lost. And so he had saved her. Stolen her into the night, where he gently bathed her, fed her from himself and held her through the torture of her rebirth. He'd battled her when she'd been insane with hunger, intent on drinking the town dry, starting with her parents and the minister who had condemned her human soul to hell. He, together with his mates, had taught her, encouraged her, and comforted her as if she were a toddler, pushing her boundaries as a newborn vampire, exploring her strengths and battling the ornery chip on her shoulder that both her human and vampire lives had left her with.

Willa's heart had swelled in her chest, yearning for Saskia's family to return from work. No matter how dangerous it may seem, she was overwhelmed with the urge to throw her arms around the trio with gratitude. She knew even now, that they'd saved the only person she'd ever love. Saved Saskia, over a hundred years ago, so that she could love her now.

Now as the sun edged higher in the sky, all Willa wanted was to stay right where she was, sitting on Saskias chaise, watching the bush come alive as they continued to explore each other's lives. The family had arrived home not long before the sky started to lighten. Full of energy after a night performing, the trio had called cheery greetings and promises of family time in the future, before hustling each other through to one of the hidden wings of the house, away from the large open room Willa and Saskia had shared all night.

Saskia had giggled... Giggled! When had she ever giggled? She was a vampire, vampires didn't giggle. Ok, well maybe Hayden did, but she was a blonde cheerleader type and giggling seemed to be a leftover trait from her long ago human life. Just as the love of sunlight was for Saskia. But when Saskia found herself giggling and explaining to Willa that her family were usually quite affectionate, disgustingly randy was the exact description, after a good performance and a tasty breakfast, Willa couldn't help but join her. Blushing hotly and giggling like a schoolgirl as she wondered what it would be like to be dragged, lip-locked into Saskia's bedroom. If Saskia took her in hand right now, she doubted she'd resist, no matter how tired she was.

And she was tired. So tired that if she blinked slowly it was likely she'd fall asleep in the fraction of a second her eyes were closed. Her brain and heart were desperate to stay right where she was and let life go on without her on the other side of the glass. She'd stay in this little UV proof, vampire bubble with Saskia. However, no matter what she desired, her body was screaming for sleep. Did vampires sleep? Did they need to sleep during the day or their eyeballs started bleeding and they shrivelled up like prunes? Gazing at Saskia's clear, garnet coloured eyes, she saw no hint of bleeding, though she did see desire, hunger and steely self-control. She was mesmerized and couldn't look away, couldn't even blink... Until she did, swaying slightly as her exhaustion attempted to take over the minute her eye lids drooped.

"You need to sleep." Saskia's voice was low and husky. "I'd invite you to stay, but I'm not sure you'd get any rest. And to be honest, I can't guarantee I won't accidentally make you my breakfast snack."

Willa's eyes widened at Saskias words. While she was all for the 'not getting any rest' according to her hyped up hormones, she didn't want to tempt Saskia just yet. After all, this was the first time her hormones had ever made themselves known and she kind of preferred her blood inside her. For now.

"Yeah, I guess I should go. All I intended was to try and find out how to find you... And now look, I've taken up your whole night. I'm sure you had plans." Willa Shrugged. "As much as I'd love to hang out all day, I'm knackered. I need my bed and a whole lotta beauty sleep. You're lucky, you don't need beauty sleep..."

Gasping at Saskia's smile, Willa realized her brain was quickly disconnecting from her mouth again.

"Oh, I'm sorry. I meant that in a good way. You know you're gorgeous. A goddess. A dark angel. I didn't mean that you don't need to sleep or anything... Do you sleep? I mean, I get that you're dead-ish, but do you sleep during the day? Do you have a coffin? How does all that work? Oh my god! OK, I'll just shut up now."

Saskia laughed softly, standing and helping a weary and rambling Willa to her feet.

"You don't need beauty sleep any more than I do, but you do need sleep, Willa. And yes, vampires sleep. We don't have to, but it helps the daylight hours go quicker and kill some time. Not that I've slept much recently. I've been too obsessed with finding you. Though today, well I might take a nap. Hopefully, I'll get to see you in my dreams."

They stood a moment, hands intertwined, just smiling stupidly at each other, both reluctant for the night to end.

"I'd walk you to your car, but you know... Sunburn and all," Saskia murmured. "Are you ok to drive? I mean if you're too tired, I can go crash in with the others. You can sleep in my bed and I promise that my family will keep you safe from... Well, whatever I'm tempted to do. I don't want you to drive if you're too tired."

Willa was sorely tempted. She dithered for a moment. She was tired, but she also knew she was ok to drive. At this hour the traffic would be light and did she really want to test Saskia? Hell yes!

Her teeth caught her lip as she worked to force out the words she didn't want to say. Saskia reached out and ran her thumb gently over Willa's bottom lip, freeing it.

"I'm the only one who's going to be nibbling on that lip," she whispered.

"I... I... Ok." Willa breathed. "Um, I better go. I'll be fine driving home, don't worry. I'm going to have to call in sick to work today though, but I don't care. It is totally worth it to spend time with you."

Saskia nodded and then was gone in a flash and returned just as quickly. A small scrap of paper crumpled into Willa's hands as Saskia backed her towards the front door.

"Call me when you get home so I know you're safe." Saskia urged, leaning in and feathering Willa's lips with a soft kiss that made her tingle.

Mutely nodding, Willa waited until Saskia had retreated toward the back of the house before opening the door to a gloriously sunny day and making her way back to reality.

CHAPTER 7

"Oh my god Sass, it's raining cats and dogs out there!" Willa shook her drenched hair, spraying droplets of water in all directions. "I'm lucky the tram stop is right outside, or I may have had to swim home."

Saskia smiled as she wrapped her arms around Willa, kissing her damp skin.

"I still hate you getting home so late, no matter how close the tram stop is. But you're here now and that's all that counts. I have a surprise for you."

Willa wrung the rain from her long hair and shrugged out of her soaked jacket.

"How long ago did you get here?" She queried, disappearing to strip off her wet clothes. "You're not working tonight?"

Saskia slouched against the kitchen island, her eyes burning as Willa reappeared from the bathroom wearing slouchy sweatpants and an old, soft t-shirt. Though Willa looked pretty damn hot in her heels and professional office skirts with her hair tamed in a bun, she looked even sexier in her favourite comfy clothes, hair tumbling in wild lavender waves down her back. Saskia's fingers itched to run through the waves and gently scratch Willa's head while she kissed her silly. It always made her Willa sigh in the most magical way.

"I beat the rain by about 10 minutes. As soon as the sun set I headed over." Saskia explained, pulling Willa to her, kissing away the last raindrops as they ran from her hair.

Willa moaned quietly as Saskia's lips traced her neck to her collarbone, her tongue lapping up raindrops as she went.

"Sassi," she panted, fighting to keep her eyes from rolling back into her head. She loved the feel of Saskia's lips, so firm, so soft, so... So, tempting. "Work? Babe?"

Forcing herself to pull away, Saskia steeled herself. Her self control was getting weaker and weaker by the day. It had been almost a month since they'd found each other and they'd been the most wonderful, torturous days in her entire existence. The moment the sun set that first day, Saskia had covered the kilometres between the mountain and Willa's tiny, city flat in record time. Willa had managed a few hours of Saskia dream-filled slumber and had been trying to work up the courage to call Saskia when a timid knock at her door brought her dream girl directly into her home.

They'd picked up their conversation right where they'd left off and they'd not run out of words yet.

Saskia found that the more time she spent with Willa, the more she craved. Both time and woman. Willas skin was so soft, it was made to be kissed and caressed. Her blood positively sang, her heart rate kicking up a notch or two every time she came close to Saskia. Which made the torture all the worse and even sweeter. That she had such an effect on Willa had Saskia feeling like her dead heart had restarted and beat in time with Willa'. The tempting warmth of her sweet-smelling blood made her mouth water and her fangs ache as she fought to contain them.

Now, after a month, she was ready. Her control was concrete. She hoped. And if she didn't give into temptation soon, well she shuddered to think what the outcome might be when she eventually did. She only hoped that Willa was ready too. Saskia thought she was, but she couldn't be sure. After all, according to Willa, this was something completely new to her in so many ways. A vampire relationship – sure, they weren't particularly common between other species, so that might be a concern to Willa. And also, despite a few flings with uninteresting males in the past, Saskia was sure that this would be Willa's first foray into the female arena. It was a whole new ballpark so to speak.

"No work." Saskia's voice was shaky as she whispered against Willa's mouth. "I have a treat for you. Well, hopefully for us. But mostly for you."

Willas face shone with delight as she leaned slightly away from Saskias oh so distracting lips.

"A surprise? Can I have it now? Pleeeeease? I couldn't need a treat more, today was absolutely crap. Everything I worked on yesterday, I had to redo today because the initial tests were inconclusive. A whole day wasted when I could have spent it doing so much more enjoyable things." Willa huffed.

Saskia raised an eyebrow and smirked slightly.

"Oh yeah? Like what?" She queried easing her fingers through Willa's hair, her nails lightly scratching her scalp.

"Um… Well, I, umm. Lots of things I guess. Oh, that's so good." Willa sighed Saskia gently suckled on her earlobe as her nails continued their work.

"What else is enjoyable?" Saskia prompted again, knowing full well the effect she was having on Willa. Waiting, breathlessly for the answer she truly wanted.

"Umm, enjoyable? I'd rather be home. With you. You're the more enjoyable I'd like to be doing…"

Another small moan escaped Willa as Saskia smiled against her neck, licking her way along that oh so tempting vein that was fluttering wildly beneath her ministrations.

"Do you mean that? About me? You know. Us?" Saskia whispered huskily.

"More than anything." Willa panted. "I mean if that's ok? I've never… You know? Been with a woman before. Or a vampire. I'm not sure how it works or anything. But I want you. You make me burn inside whenever you're around. No one has ever made me feel like this… Show me. Show me how to love you."

Saskia disentangled herself from Willa's embrace, leading her into the kitchen.

"First, I feed you," Saskia murmured, holding a slice of banana cake to Willa's lips.

The moan of appreciation that followed did nothing for her self control, she could only hope that the banana did its job.

Willa's tongue writhed around Saskia's fingers, cracking her steely resolve just a little.

"Ok," she demurred "I've had some, and while I always love your cooking, I know what I'd rather be doing right now…"

"Cake," Saskia encouraged, offering another slice. "It's important…"

Willa gently suckled Saskia's frosting covered fingers, delighting in the gasp it produced together with the flustered look on the vampires normally composed face.

"Cake. So. Important" Saskia trailed some frosting across Willa's very tempting neck as she guided them to the bedroom. "I want you so badly. Not just to show you how I want to love you. You smell so, so good. I ache so badly to taste you. To drink you… When I was human I was allergic to bananas, they would make me so sick… What you eat, changes how your blood tastes. Smells. I need you to eat the cake, so I can avoid eating you."

Willa smiled, lifting her t-shirt, the lack of bra causing Saskia's dark ruby eyes to flare blood red as though lit from within.

"Maybe I want you to eat me," she sighed raggedly, taking Saskias hands and running them across her chest. "Maybe I want to eat you too…"

"Ok, so the banana worked. Barely." Saskia panted, snuggling into Willa's side her head resting on her chest. The perky nipple right in front of her was oh so tempting right now. But Willa was on the verge of complete collapse. Her enthusiasm and stamina and ability to ingest the entire banana cake over the course of the previous six hours certainly made up for any lack of experience that Willa may have been concerned about. If anything, it was Saskia who'd finally had to call an end to Willas many novel attempts at overpowering the vampire and having her way with her, before the witch passed out altogether.

"I managed not to eat you… Well, I did eat you, and trust me you are delicious. But you're still alive with all your blood on the inside." Saskia chuckled, absently tracing patterns across Willa's skin.

"I certainly ate my fill and your cake was pretty good too." Willa shivered, tilting Saskia's face into her gentle kiss. "I still want you. Like, right now! But I'm so tired I can't move and everything aches – I'm pretty sure parts of me that I never knew existed ache, but in a really good way."

"Sleep my love, There's still a few hours before I have to get home. Time enough for me to try to not kill you again."

Willa sighed. If only they could stay right here forever. Wrapped up in each other. If only she could convince Saskia to use those glorious, long fangs on her. Every time they scratched lightly over her skin, a coil inside her tightened just a little more. And while Saskia had inspired orgasm after mind-blowing orgasm, that coil was still there, tense and tight within her.

CHAPTER 8

"Hey, Hayden? Can I ask you something?" Willa paused in the open doorway to Hayden's music room. While spending time with Saskia's family had become common place over the past six months, it had always been as a group combination that included Sass.

"Sure sweetie, come on in. Where's Sass? It's not often I see you without your shadow." Hayden beckoned Willa to join her on the couch.

"Sorry, am I interrupting?" Willa indicated to the sheet music scattered on the floor.

Hayden grimaced and patted the seat.

"Not at all. I'm stuck. I've been lying here for hours trying to get the flow right for the new melody, but it just won't come. I could really use a break. And you seem to have abandoned your job as Chief Taste Tester…"

Willa giggled. The vampire family had dubbed her Chief Taste Tester because One And Only Taste Tester And Food Eater was too much of a mouthful. Ha! What would they know about a mouthful? It's not like they were being served up gourmet meals on a daily basis. And if she had to eat one more banana-based desert, no matter how decadent she might just develop an allergy to them herself… On second thoughts, as sick as she was of banana, the benefits definitely outweighed her growing aversion in the long run.

"Nope, I made a run for it. Sass had scones in the oven and is fitting Klaus and Daniel for their Madonna bras. They're looking kinda cool, though Klaus's 5 o'clock shadow doesn't take well to make-up."

Willa sank onto the end of the couch, keeping a careful distance between Hayden and herself. Though she knew that she was completely safe with Saskia's family, she also didn't want to cause discomfort to them by being too close. They'd all attested to how good she smelled, though they also reassured her that she wasn't as tempting to them as she was to Saskia.

"Um, I wanted to talk to you without Sass if that's ok? I wanted to ask you something and… Well, I… I don't know. I just feel weird bringing it up with her or the guys."

"Oooo! This sounds juicy. Whatever it is, it'll stay between us. Ask away, sweety."

Hayden squeezed Willa's hand in encouragement and settled back into the cushions.

"Soooo, um. Well, I was wondering about you. You and the guys. The three of you?"

Willas face burned as she stammered. She knew what she wanted to know, she just didn't know how to ask.

Hayden's brows raised in surprise.

"You want to know about the three of us? Our history? How we came to be vampires? Or the three of us - How we came to be three? Sweetie, while I'll gladly tell you both stories, I've gotta warn you, if a threesome is what you're interested in, I don't think that's up Saskia's alley. I mean she'd do anything for you, no matter what. But she's just not into multiples."

Willa couldn't help drawing a sharp breath that stuck in her throat. Coughing and choking on the air and her embarrassed laugh, she eyed the open door debating if she could make a run for it or should she just pray the ground opened up and swallowed her whole.

"No... No not that! I mean, it's obviously perfect for you. Daniel, Klaus and you are perfect, and I couldn't imagine one of you without the other two. But I'm with Sass and she's more than enough woman for me. I've never wanted anyone else and never will. But that's what I want to know about? How did you know? The three of you?"

Willas head dropped, she just couldn't form the words if she had to look at Hayden's inquisitive face.

"How did you know you were meant for each other? Mates? How did you know?" She whispered.

Hayden shot from the couch, softly closing the door and returning in the blink of an eye.

"Sweetie? You want to know about mates? Those two lug-heads wearing sequined bra's out there have excellent hearing and would have a few choice jokes for you, given the chance... So you and Sass? You're really that serious?"

Willa shrugged, her head felt so hot it might burst into flames. Not ideal around a vampire. She hung her head, focusing hard on the cushion she pulled into her lap. Though it offered no protection, it was nice to have a shield of sorts.

"Willa? Do you think that Saskia is your mate? Does she too? Have you talked about this?"

Willa's shoulders again shrugged slightly as she slowly shook her head.

"That's what I wanted to talk to you about. I love Sass. I love Sass with everything in me. When it's daytime and I have to go to work, I can't concentrate. All I do is think about her. About us. When she's near me, it's like every tiny cell inside me comes alive. I can feel my magic sparking like electricity in my mind. I can feel my heart racing and all I want is to be close to her. Be, you know... With her. If I could I'd climb inside her so we could be one person."

Hayden's lips drew up taking in the fire that burned in Willa's eyes as she talked about Saskia. This little witch was so passionate about her sister, Hayden recognized the feelings she described. She too had felt them. The moment that Klaus and Daniel had entered her village, almost a thousand years ago she'd felt it. She too hadn't known what it meant. She'd been alone her entire afterlife, and most of her life before that. She'd never known another vampire. Never been taught. The one who had turned her was long gone before she regained her senses. She'd been so young back then, both as a human and a vampire. Her childhood human friends still lived their adult lives within the village. The army that had ruled over them since before she was human born still camped in the fields, providing easy earnings and eating for her by night. She was an innocent to the vampire world, despite draining soldiers regularly. She remembered the burning that ran through her veins when she first laid eyes on her men. So tall, so magnetic. The pull to them so overwhelming. She'd been sure they would make the ultimate meal. A gourmet banquet after filling her afterlife with mere snacks. How wrong she'd been. How right she'd been. The moment she launched herself at Daniel through the darkness, Klaus was there. Holding her in arms as strong as iron and yet so gently. He'd whispered words in her ear she had no understanding of. But the moment their eyes met, she'd seen the fire. The very fire that burned inside her, burned within his eyes. And as Klaus held her, the desire to tear herself apart, to drink him in, to drink in the other man with the smouldering ember eyes drove her insane... Then Daniel bit her and the whole world stopped. Every moment of confusion she'd ever had, every ounce of loneliness disappeared from her life.

The world suddenly made sense as the trio fed on each other.

Willa's breath came fast and shallow as Hayden described her mating. Those feelings were still as overwhelming and strong this moment as they were so long ago. The passion they felt for each other grew stronger with each passing year. The knowledge that they could never, would never, live without each other. All three would perish should one perish. It was a given. It was inevitable. It was a privilege and their ultimate desire. They'd never be alone. They'd never be apart. They would forever be three.

That's what she wanted, Willa thought. That's what she felt for Saskia. Without Sass, there was no Willa. Nodding quietly Willa contemplated all that Hayden had said. Of one thing she was absolutely sure now, Saskia was her destined mate. The one being to ever exist that her heart beat for. But what now? Could a vampire and a witch even be mates? Could they find a place to exist together when their worlds were as separate as night and day?

"Willa, you'll find a way," Hayden murmured drawing Willa into a warm embrace. "You two are meant to be and so you will be. Speaking for my family, you not only have our blessing but there has been a place for you right here since that full moon party."

Willa smile trembled as she wiped tears from her eyes.

"Sorry, it's just…" Again she didn't have the words to describe what she felt inside.

"It's a lot. It's everything. And you know what, sweetie? The only thing missing that would make it perfect is my men in ugly bridesmaid frocks."

Willa snorted loudly, nodding. That would indeed be perfect.

"Hayden, you don't know where I could get ahold of a truck load of fresh lavender and strawberries do you?"

CHAPTER 9

"Hey, babe, Hayden and the guys are heading away for the weekend to visit some friends up near Canberra. So we've got the house to ourselves this weekend. We can do the full moon gathering and then... Well, I'm sure we can find a few ways to worship the moon just the two of us."

Willa fought to hide the excitement in her voice. While she was always more than happy to have alone time with Saskia, with or without a silver moon overhead, she didn't want to give away her secret just yet. Not when she and Hayden had gone to so much effort to arrange everything.

"That's no prob, Sass. I'm just in from work. It'll take me a bit to change and pack a few things then I'll meet you there if that's ok? I want to drop in on Ella before everyone starts to party. It feels like ages since we've had time to catch up without half the community dropping by."

Saskia laughed at the other end of the phone.

"That's what you get for hooking up with one of the hot new vamps in town. Even supes love titilation babe."

Willa giggled. Saskia was right, dating a vampire was cause for a whole lot of community interest and gossip… Just wait till they saw what she had planned.

"I know love. Of course, while you are the hottest vamp in town, you're also one of only four so they'd gossip whether we were together or not. I'm sure they'll always find something juicy about us to discuss. Ok, I've gotta run if I don't want to keep a lovely lady waiting tonight."

Willa danced with excitement as she untangled herself from the phone cord and replaced the receiver. In reality, she was all ready to go, she'd just been waiting on Saskia's phone call, prompted by an accommodating Hayden. All she needed to do now was have a chat with Ella and she'd be all set. Everything was ready at the bonfire. With Saskia's families assistance, she'd managed to avoid her all week while she prepared. It was killing her, for them to be apart. She'd been useless at work, making mistakes and spacing out while she went over her plans again and again. She'd mixed and brewed potions and lotions especially for tonight. She'd discussed what she needed with a warlock who dabbled in the darker side of life. And she'd called in numerous favours, begged and pleaded to ensure the attendance of the high priestess. This month's full moon would be gossiped about for years to come. Of that she was sure.

"Ella, I'd love your blessing tonight. But you need to understand, with or without it I'm going through with it. This is everything I want in life. Everything I will ever need. Please, please be happy for me. Support me. Give me your blessing."

Ella sighed. Willa could tell she wasn't happy, sitting at the kitchen table, unconsciously fidgeting with the flower vase. She really wanted her grandmothers' blessing. For her to stand by her side, before the entire community and show her support. Saskia's family were behind her 100%, and lord knows she wished hers was too.

"What about your parents my love? Do they know? Have you spoken with them or do you plan to just spring this on them after the fact? You know how they feel about the community. About me, our life… Do you really expect them to be happy about this?"

Tears brimmed in Willa's eyes. These were questions she could answer without any doubts. Despite their differences and her parents steadfast rejection of the supernatural community, including Ella, Willa had hoped that they'd bend just a little for their daughter. They would not.

"They know." Her voice cracked as she struggled to keep the pain at bay. "I had dinner this week with mum and dad. We talked. I told them about Sass. I wanted them to meet her. I thought, if they could just meet her, see how wonderful she is and how happy I am, then it'd be ok. I was wrong. Mum was crying, she kept going on and on about how they were relying on me for grandchildren. I told them, I love her and she loves me. We are destined. Fated mates. That's what really set them off. I'm still not sure what they were more against. The fact that I'm in love with a vampire, or that I'm in love with a woman… Either way, dad told me I had a choice to make. If I wanted to remain part of the family, I'd break up with Saskia. But if I insist on tying myself to an undead lesbian then I'd be as dead to them as she already is… I had to leave when he said that. I just couldn't stand there and listen to him talk about Sass that way."

Willas head dropped as tears spilled down her cheeks.

"I went back the next morning. I thought once they had time to calm down and think about it, then maybe I could reason with them. Ella. Dad had the locks changed. My key wouldn't even fit. I could see them both in the kitchen when I went to the back door, but they just ignored me. Sat there drinking tea until I went away."

Ella's heart broke for her granddaughter. As much as she knew Willa's parents refused the legacy of their family, she never thought they'd deny their beautiful, loving daughter in such a hurtful way. Love was love, whether between a man, a woman, multiple partners or varying species. Sure, suburbia was still scandalized when it came to gay relationships, but to declare your child dead simply because of who she loved… Well, that was unforgivable.

"Oh, my precious child. Of course I support you. How could I not? You are my family and I am yours and now Saskia is family. And the others too. Your parents are insane with their prejudices but we are gaining four new family members all of whom you will love with all that you are. I just worry, is all. I worry for you both – Saskia and you, my darling. I truly believe you are fated mates, but your journey won't be easy. There are many who will not accept a vampire and a witch. There will be so many roadblocks in your way. Something as simple as spending time together will be a struggle… She's a creature of the night and you, my girl, are a sun worshipper. Love can overcome a lot, but your girlfriend bursting into flames on a beach holiday is not one of them."

Willa couldn't help but snigger at Ella's irreverent humour. Yes, there would be no honeymoon on the Gold Coast in their future that's for sure.

"I not only give you my blessing my love, but I'd be honoured if you'd let me stand with you. Let the entire mountain know that love is what counts and the rest… Well, I'm sure you can work that out."

Drying her eyes on the back of her hand, Willa smiled bravely.

"I have a plan and I'd love you to stand with me. All I need now is Saskia."

Glancing around the gathering crowd Saskia was desperate to find Willa. They hadn't spent any time together in a week and it was tearing her apart inside. More than once she'd almost made a dash for the door while the sun was still above the horizon, desperate to just feel her near. Willa living in the city while she spent her days here on the mountain was something that needed to change. Sooner rather than later. Somehow, the universe was determined to keep them apart, between Willa working extra hours, late into the evening, and the family requiring her presence for some trivial matter or another at the theatre each night. She'd been confined to phone calls for days. And while a phone call was better than nothing and reassured her that Willa wasn't pulling away, they did nothing to stave off the hunger that was growing inside her. She needed her woman, and she needed her now.

The bonfire burned high as the Fae danced and fluttered about, lighting the sky with trails of their magic. Strangely, Saskia spotted her family the moment she'd arrived. According to Klaus, they'd decided to celebrate the full moon with their community for a short while before running up to Canberra. A medicine man sat in deep discussion with an old warlock. The little Fae girls from the nursery were creating blossom archways beneath the gum trees while their parents stood in respectful attendance of a high priestess. For a small mountain community, they were certainly an eclectic and prestigious gathering this month.

Then suddenly, there she was. Her angel. And she was an angel, especially tonight. The lavender twisted and weaved through her matching hair. The long white dress she wore, baring her neck and shoulders in such a tantalising way. My goodness, Saskia just wanted to sink her fangs into her girl. The bare feet, gliding across the fallen leaves, ready for dancing the night away. And the strange, quirk of her mouth. That smile had Saskia curious as to what secrets Willa still held within her. Ella was beaming beside Willa as they crossed the clearing. Ever animated at these gatherings, Ella looked like she'd been smoking a few too many of her herbs tonight.

Willa's eyes sparked as Saskia drew her into her arms, lifting her feet from the ground as she took her lips in a searing kiss that left her breathless. It physically pained her to disentangle herself and step back from her beloved dark goddess slightly but it must be done for what came next.

With a twirl of a finger, Willa threw a little magic above the gathered group, prompting a hush as the crowd registered something special was to occur.

"Saskia. I love you more than I could ever have imagined possible. You are my life. My everything. The thought of us not being together... Well, it just kills me. You are the reason my heart beats. My magic flows stronger in your presence. You are my fate. My mate…" Willa swallowed down the emotions that were bubbling in her chest and dropped to her knees. "Saskia? Will you marry me? Will you join me as my blessed mate?"

Saskia's mouth dropped open. If she were still possible of crying, there would be tears of joy flowing like a river right now at the sight of her beloved, kneeling at her feet, offering her glittering gold ring inlaid with rose quartz. Why was she on her knees? Willa was her fate. The entire reason she had spent a century alone, without light or passion in her life. She'd been waiting for this moment. Willa didn't need to beg.

Scooping her up Saskia smiled as she peppered Willas face with dainty kisses.

"My love, we are always going to be together. Forever. I can't believe you beat me to the punch here. I was going to ask you, but I was still trying to work stuff out…"

Willa's face lit up like a sunrise. She raised her hand and twirled the ring before Saskia's eyes.

"So… Is that a yes?" she queried.

"Yes? YES!" Saskia squealed as Willa slid the ring onto her finger. "Yes, yes, yes, yes yes… But how? I mean, I love you and I want you forever but that's what I was trying to work out… How? You're human. Sort of. Well, for the purposes of life expectancy anyway. And while I fully intend to greet the sun a final time when you eventually leave me alone on this earth, I'd rather it resemble my lifespan more than a humans. And how are we to live? I'm a night owl. I love you and I'm desperate to be tied to you but I worry…"

Willa smiled as the cheers allowed only her to hear Saskias entire response. She knew her brooding, overthinking lover would have concerns. After all, she had the same ones. But she'd come prepared to deal with some of them anyway. The rest, she and Ella would work to find a resolution as soon as possible.

"Shh, babe. It's ok, I understand. The most important thing is you and I. Us. Together. That's what's important. That and you said YES!" Willa kissed Saskia deeply, her tongue playing along the length of those wonderful fangs.

"Fated mates. Tied for life… I have a plan. There's someone I want you to meet."

CHAPTER 10

Leading Saskia across the clearing, Willa smiled as they were both congratulated over and over by those gathered. Any concerns with regards to the community accepting their union were erased entirely.

"There's someone I'd like you to meet. Now promise me, you'll hear us out before you make a decision... I hope that you'll understand what I've found. But I will understand and honour you should you not agree... Either way, we will be tied. Very soon." Willa was nervous now. Excited to find out what Saskia's reaction would be. Would she accept the blessing on offer? Would she still agree to be tied? Tonight?

"Sassi, babe. I'd like you to meet Gruphig Mita. Lord Gruphig, I'm pleased to present my fiancé and mate – Saskia"

To Saskia's surprise, Willa bowed slightly as she introduced her to the old warlock she'd noticed earlier. He must be important to rate such a formal introduction.

"Pleased to meet you, sir," she smiled, threading an arm around her woman as she held out a hand to the warlock.

His large fingers grasped hers as he turned her hand palm up and inhaled the skin deeply.

"Hmm, yes. I believe it will happen." He murmured taking Willa's hand and placing it in Saskia's and inhaling again. "Yes. This is good. You are perfectly matched. There will be no problems with this. You are both strong. Your magic feeds each other and your joining will only serve to make you stronger still. Hmmm, yes this is good. This is good."

Withdrawing her hand, Saskia turned to Willa confused.

"What's this, Will?"

Smiling, Willa settled Gruphig back onto his seat and turned to Saskia.

"I love you so much Sass, and I know that we're going to have a wonderful life together. But I understand your concerns about our future. I have those concerns too. I mean, it's not exactly common place, a witch and a vampire. It's nothing that anyone around here has ever heard of. So I had to do a little research. And you know how good I am at research. It's my life!" She sighed dramatically, knowing that Saskia would understand. Despite spending all day, every day researching and calculating, it was a job she found exceptionally unfulfilling.

"Anyway, I asked around. Talked to a few people here and there. Made a whole lot of very strange phone calls and they lead me to Lord Gruphig.   He works in blood magic…"

Saskia gasped.   "He works dark?   Will, you're light. You're the sun and the moon and everything light and bright about the world and its magic…"

"Babe, it's ok. He doesn't so much work dark as he works red. Whether light or dark, the strongest magic is always blood magic. We both know that. It's why my magic is so much stronger since we've been together… You are a creature of blood.   And talking with Lord Gruphig, we realized that blood magic holds the key to our life. Our future."

"The way I understand it from your lovely witch, you intend to spend your lives tied to each other to the exclusion of all others. You believe you are fated."

The warlock looked quite bored as he spoke, as though their love was of no consequence.

"Whether you are fated or not is of no interest to me. Though you are perfectly balanced and your magic is matched and feeds from the other.   Yours would be a strong and interesting joining to behold, I must say. And I can make it happen. I can join you. Two can become one. One life, one existence for all time…"

Saskia glanced at Willa, her confusion only growing stronger as the warlock spoke vaguely.

"What's he talking about Willa? What's going on?"

Willa smiled as she grasped Saskias hands and kissed them gently.

"Lord Gruphig has a way for us to be joined. Truly joined. Not just tied for my lifetime. But joined for eternity. As I said, he works in blood magic and he has a potion that when mixed with our blood, will join our lives – literally. For as long as you live, I will live; and as long as I live, so will you. Our blood, our lives, our magic, our very existence will be joined, combined and will become one. You never again need to have thoughts of meeting the sun when I die. I'll always be with you. As long as you are immortal, I will be too…"

A spark of hope sprung inside Saskia and quickly grew inside her heart, fuelled by her love and the thought of never having to be without her beloved Willa.

"But how? What will it take? And how do we know it will work?"

The warlocks expression turned dark at her doubt.

"I am so much older than you, young vampire. You need to respect my magic. I am the oldest and strongest warlock in Australia. I have been here weaving my magic and creating blood potions since the days of the original inhabitants. Respect and trust in me when I say, my magic never fails. If I say I can join you for eternity, then that's exactly what I can do… And all it will take is a drop of blood. My potion is ready, all it needs is a single drop of fresh blood from each of you. When you vow your existence to each other and are tied, you will each drink of the potion and you will be joined completely."

"That simple? Why? What's in it for you?" Saskia queried. She'd found that things that seemed to be too good to be true usually were.

"Ahh, there is nothing simple about it. It has taken me many weeks to prepare the potion for your witch, and it will only have the desired result if the blood is given freely by each. As to why? There is nothing 'in it for me'. I like your young witch. She respects her elders and those more powerful than she… After all, she has chosen to be tied to you has she not? And I understand the desire to never be without your mate, your family. My magic costs no money, though all magic has a price. I know not what that price may be for you two lovely children. Only time and the magic know. It may be a millennia or it may be tomorrow when the price is revealed. But no matter the cost, you will remain within each other until the end of time."

Saskia stood, silently considering his words. She could truly have Willa forever. She would never grow old. Never die. They would be tied for eternity. Bound by their love, their magic and their blood.

Turning to Willa, her face lit like the heavens at sunrise she pulled her into her arms and kissed her passionately.

"I want you forever Willa. I trust in the magic." She whispered breathlessly. "How soon can we organize a wedding?"

Willa giggled as Saskia's family stepped forward, bearing a long garment bag.

"Umm, how about right now babe? Everyone we love is here. Hayden has a gown. The High Priestess has agreed to tie us. Lord Gruphig has his potion, and we have your house to ourselves this weekend..."

"Give me five minutes..." Saskia urged turning to the warlock. "One drop? That's all you need? From each of us?"

At his confirming nod, she lifted her wrist to her fangs and froze as her gaze moved to Willa, knife in hand.

"Umm, maybe it'd be better if we did this separately. You smell all too delicious tonight my love and I'd hate to accidentally eat you before I make you immortal."

Willa chuckled, that was her woman. Always so concerned about her safety. Always so afraid she'd be tempted to bite her. Well if Willa had her way, she'd be doing some biting of her own very soon.

"Go dress gorgeous," she directed. "I'll take care of my part while you're gone. And then we can get married!" Willa squealed with excitement.

Turning, Saskia followed Hayden and Aine to the Fae house in the gully, to dress. And though she could no longer see the bonfire or the clearing, she could smell Willa's blood the moment the knife pierced her skin, causing her fangs to lengthen and ache with desire.

Willa's breath stuck in her throat as her heart swelled to a bursting point at the sight of Saskia approaching. The whole world dropped away and all that was left was Saskia. She was an absolute vision. An angel that fell from the heavens. A true goddess walking the earth, walking to her destiny at Willa's side as she looked on in breathless rapture.

Hayden had been in charge of wedding attire and if she ever decided to give up the life of a musician, she had a promising career as a stylist to the stars ahead of her. While Willa liked her lace, boho-chic gown, Saskia's outfit was the stuff of legends. It would be spoken of in hushed, envious tones for years to come. In the human world, Saskia's gown would have more media coverage than any royal wedding. As she glided across the grass, the firelight painted her fitted ivory satin gown with dancing golden light. Her hair spilled down her back, like a dark waterfall. And her ruby eyes flared with blood boiling with desire as her heated gaze met Willa's awe-filled eyes.

It took everything within her, and Ella's steady hand on her arm to stop Willa from sprinting to her woman's side. Would Saskia consent to wearing only this gown for the rest of their lives? As Klaus and Daniel came into view trailing Saskia Willa really hoped someone had a camera handy. While she would never forget the sight of her wife on their wedding day, her goddess needed to be immortalised in print. Plus the sight of her family frocked up in full, sequined, drag queen regalia carrying bouquets of wattle blossom – well that required evidence for future blackmail purposes. The family photograph taken today would certainly be like no other.

As Saskia finally joined her under the floral arbour that little Rhiannon and Neela had created, Willa could not stay her hands any longer and reached for her beloved. The moment their fingers met her heart skipped a beat and then began to race. In this moment, nothing mattered. Not her family. Not the worrying semantics of navigating life together. Nothing mattered, only the goddess before her and the fact that their souls were about to combine for all eternity.

"I bind you together. Fated mates, souls tied never to separate. Your union is destined, blessed by your magic, your family, your community and the gods and goddesses who watch over us all."

The soft rope twined around Saskia and Willa's joined hands, the knot magically tied as the high priestess blessed them and bound their lives by ancient Wiccan handfasting with a gentle smile.

The old warlock stepped forward and offered up a carved wooden chalice. Saskia's breath stuck in her throat as the perfume of Willa's blood rose from the liquid within.

Willa's smile outshone the brilliant stars above as she took a sip and licked the rose coloured potion from her lips with a satisfied hum.

"It tastes like you," she whispered. "You know? Right before you… You know?"

Saskia tried not to laugh. Trust her girl to air that little gem to the entire supernational community.

Bringing the cup to her mouth Saskia drank deeply, there was no way any was going to waste a drop and risk the potion not working.

Her eyes rolled back in her head as the heady scent of Willa filled her head, her lungs. That single drop of blood packed one hell of a punch, just as she'd always been afraid it would. There was nothing she'd ever tasted that was as sweet. It was like drinking pure magic and all she wanted was more. Hopefully, they had plenty of bananas at home for their honeymoon.

"You are bound. Tied by magic, joined by blood until time itself ends. She is yours and you are hers. Your lives are now within. Two are one, for now, and forever. Never to be parted, never to fade."

At Gruphig's words, Saskia scooped Willa into her arms and kissed her with a passion that burned like wildfire within her. As Willa's heart kicked into overdrive, the scent of her blood overwhelmed Saskia. It was all just too much. She had to have her... Now.

In the blink of an eye, the brides disappeared from the bonfire. Leaving the wedding guests to party the night away without them.

The tattered scraps of wedding gown fabric created a Hansel and Grettel trail from the full moon party up the mountain to Saskia's bedroom. Running her tongue over Willa's ribs, Saskia groaned, wrapping her fists around the bedhead and forcing herself off her wife who whimpered at the loss.

"Sweet heart, you smell way, way too tempting right now... How long does it take for that immortal thing to kick in? Did Gruphig say? Because you smell like food... I mean you always smell like food, but tonight you really smell like food. Like the cakes that I used to sneak from the kitchen as a human."

Willa fearlessly broached the void, entwining her arms and legs around any part of Saskia's smooth, marble body she could reach.

"That's because I do research, my wife. The devil is in the details and I remembered you mentioned that lavender honey and strawberry shortcake were your favourite foods when you were human. So I might have spent the last week eating them for every meal. And I may have cooked up a lotion and bath oil to bathe in and dab on all the artery points described in my anatomy books"

Saskia groaned as Willa kissed her way down her neck. She could hear her heart pounding wildly, pumping strawberry and honey-scented blood to every minuscule capillary in her Wiccan minx's body.

"You're killing me! I'm trying so hard not to bite you here. I don't want to hurt you…"

Willa smiled, gently stroking Saskias fangs with a fingertip.

"Maybe that's the point. Maybe I want you to bite me… I've wanted it for so long. I want these. They're mine now. My wedding present to myself." She whispered huskily. "And if you're not going to give me what I want. If you're not going to bite me… Well, I'll just have to bite you."

Faster than Saskia even realized possible, Willa brought her lips to Saskia's neck and bite down as hard as she could. While her blunt human teeth were no match for Saskia's impervious vampire skin, they did manage to tear through the last shred of her self control. The last fragments of civility burned away and Saskia became what she'd always feared... A feral vampire, out for blood from every perfumed artery pinned beneath her.

CHAPTER 11

"If you hate your job so much, why don't you just quit?"

Klaus queried, his voice calm and conversational. After all, this was a topic the entire family had debated more than once over the past few years since she and Saskia had married and joined their lives.

Willa sighed. She really didn't have a valid argument as to why she stayed in her boring number crunching, chemical formula tweaking job year after year. With every day she felt a little more apathy towards her career. She'd never wanted to be a scientist, but at least when she was young and naive and believed she'd be creating life-saving medicines, it had seemed worthwhile. Now, after years of only seeing chemicals and medications as equations, the scant lustre she'd once felt had truly worn away.

"You know why Klaus. My dad wanted me to be a scientist. It's the only thing I've ever done. It's my job. What am I going to do? Quit and find another pharmaceutical company where I can do more of the same? I might as well stay put."

"But you hate your job. And not to kick you while you're down or anything, but your parents refuse to have anything to do with you… Why torture yourself day in day out for them? Why not quit the scientist life altogether and do something you truly love? Do you think we dress up in frocks and wigs every night because we are looking for approval? Hell to the no! We do it because we love it. It's fun and silly and we laugh more in one night on stage than we have for the whole of the last century. You need to do you. Be who you want. So what you want, not what your parents wanted."

Willa knew he was right. He'd said it many times, as had Hayden and Daniel and most importantly Saskia.

Her wonderful Saskia, housewife extraordinaire. Her very own Betty Crocker. Her vampire Martha Stewart. She didn't do what was 'expected' of her as a vampire. After all, she'd married a witch almost five years ago and quickly settled into married life as an old school, stay home wife. And speaking of the delicious devil, she was whipping up a tray of mini strawberry pavlovas in the kitchen at this very moment. Who would ever have guessed, someone whose diet consisted entirely of her wifes' blood would create the most amazing food Willa had ever tasted.

"I guess… I mean I know you're right Klaus. Sass and I talk about this all the time. I know I need to quit. I do hate it. And besides, sooner or later someone's going to notice that I haven't aged. I guess I can only get away with the 'good plastic surgeon and skin care regimen' for so long before people become suspicious. But what am I meant to do? It's not like I CAN do anything else."

Klaus laughed. A vampire that Willa had once thought to be so poker-faced, since she and Saskia had made their home with her family, Willa had seen the real Klaus appear. A bright, shining, smiling, joking vampire who'd could barely stand to spend a moment dwelling on life's downfalls.

"Why would you need to do anything else. Just do what you already do, what you love…"

Willa glanced from Klaus to Saskia hoping for some sort of clarification to his confusingly cryptic reply.

"Your lotions and potions, pet." Willa could hear the mixture of exasperation and amusement in his voice. "You're a witch who spends every weekend brewing lotions and potions in your cauldron… Why not put them to good use and stop stockpiling them in the hall closet? Sell them. Open a business of your own and do what you already do. What you love to do. Hell, while I indulged Saskia by building a kitchen for her hobby, I think it would be the perfect home base for Willa's Wiccan Wonders – lotions, potions and magical remedies for all your skincare needs."

Saskia's throaty chuckle filtered across the large room.

"The kitchen's sure been seeing a whole lot of action these past years, babe. Between you and I both cooking up something, we could almost open a 24/7 diner and apothecary."

"See!" Klaus popped from his seat and swung Willa around like a rag doll. "Now you have two options. Skincare or diner. Either would be a hell of a lot more fulfilling than crunching numbers in an office."

"Something to think about I guess…" Willa laughed fighting to extract herself from her brother-in-law's enthusiastic embrace.

"Sass? What do you really think I should do?"

Willa loved this time of the night. The few precious hours between night and day when she and Saskia could share some quiet time together. Time before the sun forced Willa from bed and out into the day while confining Saskia to the safety of their home. Time luxuriating in the arms of her wife.

"Well. First I think you should roll onto your back. Then I think you should put your arms above your head and hold onto the bedhead nice and tight. And then I think I should…"

"Sass! I'm serious!" Willa protested, half-heartedly pushing her away, her body begging her to submit.

"Sorry love. You're just so distracting… And tasty. I can't help my 'pavlovian' response to the appeal of meringue, strawberries and wifey."

Saskia's voice was husky and persuasive as she feathered kisses to the thundering pulse in Willa's neck.

"Babe…" Willa gasped, fighting to keep her train of thought. "Babe, please. You can eat me again later. Fuck, I'll eat a dozen more pav's and you can make a meal of me. But I… I… Awww!"

Willa's eyes flew open as Saskia's sudden withdrawal. As much as she'd protested the distraction, her blood was boiling and she was wound so tight. Their conversation could wait.

"Will. You know what I think. What I've always thought. I think your talents are wasted where you are. You're stifling your talents and I won't have anyone stifle my wife's gifts, not even my wife herself. I think. You should. Tell your boss. You quit. And we. Can spend. Our days. Cooking up lotions. And potions. And our nights. Eating sweet treats. From this. Sweet. Treat."

How Saskia managed to kiss her way from one sensitive point to another while staying on topic was a mystery to Willa, who was struggling to recall what they'd been discussing in the first place.

111

"Really Sass? Do you really think I should go for it? I guess there are plenty of little gift shops and places dotted around the mountain that I could sell to. Oh, babe." She sighed as she felt Saskia nodding against her belly. "You wouldn't get sick of me? Seeing me all day and night? Horning in on your kitchen time?"

"Willa. I want you day and night. We are joined, remember. It hurts me when we're apart. I feel hollow inside and sometimes I'm so thirsty for you it's like my throat has been cut. If I had my way, we'd never leave this bed. But then you'd still be wasting half your talents – So… I want you to quit your job and we can cook up a storm together, forever."

"Ok!" Willa gasped, stretching her arms to grasp the bedhead. "You win."

Saskia smiled. She loved a good debate with her wife. It was important for married couples to talk things out and plan a future together after all.

CHAPTER 12

"Willa? Will? Are you listening to me?" Saskia stomped through the house gathering miscellaneous debris as she went.

"Will, we can't keep going this way. You can't. I know you've got my immortality thing going for you, but you can't keep this pace up. You've been working on Lotions and Potions full time for over a year now and you're getting busier every month. It's too much for you. Trust me, I know. I can taste it inside you. You barely sleep. If you're not running all over doing deliveries, your cooking, or packing, or doing the books, or helping at the theatre. We barely have time for ourselves anymore. I miss you."

"Sass. I'm trying ok? There's just so much to do and only me during daylight hours... None of us expected Lotions and Potions to take off so quickly, but as Daniel says – Strike when the iron's hot. I'm sure it will calm down sooner or later."

Willa shrugged. Honestly, she agreed. Lotions and Potions had been an instant hit, something no one had expected or been prepared for.

"It's not just the business babe. It's everything. It's our life. I love you. I miss you. I feel like we have less time for each other now than we did back when we were first married and you had to go to work every day. And it's not just you and me. It's all of us…"

Huffing Saskia threw herself onto the bed, looking more frazzled wife and mother than vampire goddess. More and more these days she felt it too. Who knew that being the 'responsible adult' in the household of her messy, perpetually awake, active and flighty family would be resemble wrangling teenagers. In the past she'd never considered the loss of never having children, having been turned vampire so young, and now she was positive it was a yearning she would never have.

"I know sweetie. It's just that getting Lotions and Potions on its feet has taken so much time and effort. I'm sure we'll settle into some sort of routine soon. What else can we do?"

Willa crawled up the bed and spooned her sulking wife. Life hadn't exactly been easy since they'd been tied, but they'd expected that. Just not in the way it had turned out. She'd gone from being a Wiccan with a day job she hated and a vampire girlfriend she loved, to an immortal by proxy Wiccan who rarely had the time or energy to enjoy their life together.

"It's not just that," Saskia sniffed. "It's living here. My family. The theatre. The fucking sequins and glitter that's everywhere… You know I found some stuck to your boob the other night? We've gone from keeping our own spaces to living like some kind of vampire frat house. I walked in on Daniel and Klaus playing restaurant with Hayden on the kitchen island last week… With the tiramisu I made for our anniversary!"

Willa giggled. "I wondered what happened to it. I'd been looking forward to that too. Damn. Never going to be able to eat it again without that visual in my head."

It wasn't the first time that she or Saskia had stumbled across the trio 'enjoying' themselves in the shared family space of the house and it was unlikely to be the last. It was, however, the first time they'd raided the refrigerator that Saskia kept well stocked for her benefit… Of course, Hayden had gotten the idea after catching Willa and Saskia indulging in exactly the same thing a few months ago. But in their defence, they'd thought the trio were out for the night and Willa was the only family member who actually ate any of the food.

Sighing she gently climbed over Saskia to snuggle face to face.

"Yeah, we do seem to be getting a little too comfortable with each other around here in a weirdly uncomfortable way. I love us spending time as a family, I really do. That's why I love helping out at the theatre. It's so much fun. Klaus was right, I've never laughed so much as I do there. But family dinner on Monday kinda creeps me out… I mean, I know that they wouldn't eat me or anything. But being the only human sitting down at the dinner table while a bunch of vampires watch me eat is still pretty uncomfortable. You're lucky I haven't developed an eating disorder… But what else can we do? It's not like we can drop by the real estate office and ask them to find us a 3 bedroom, vampire friendly house, with a two-car garage."

Saskia rested her head on Willa's shoulder, enjoying the calm peace of just spending quiet time with her. It was such a rare treat these days.

"I guess. I just thought things would be different. You know? More 'normal' and less vampire Brady Bunch."

Willa smiled, kissing her with gentle love rather than the burning passion that normally flared. In a way, this warm, loving bubble she felt was way better.

"Let's talk it over with the others on family night. If nothing else, it'll distract them from whatever I'm eating."

"I have an idea" Daniel whispered in Willa's ear as Saskia directed the others in the kitchen clean up with the authority of a drill sergeant.

"Hmm? What sort of idea?" Willa murmured back. "Why are we whispering?"

"I have an idea for our problem. For you and Sass. Your business. Us living on top of each other. All of it. You guys need to get your own place."

Willa sighed, rolling her eyes.

"In the real world that would be perfect Dan, but there's the whole vampire thing to consider... It's not like we can just find another light-proof house built into the side of a mountain. I'm pretty sure this is a one of a kind around here."

Daniel laughed quietly.

"You're very right little lady. This house IS a one of a kind. And so shall yours be... Come, I want to show you."

Glancing towards the kitchen, Saskia's full attention was focused on her slaves. By the sounds of it, she'd be in full-blown homemaker mode for hours as she whipped her family and the house into shape. Hayden was going to regret volunteering them to do whatever Saskia wanted to help with the upkeep. Willa followed Daniel out into the darkness and down the mountain to the Fae Nursery.

"What do you think?"

"Of what?" Willa was confused. Why were they standing on the side of the road by the nursery in the middle of the night?

"Of that," Daniel responded pointing to the old two-story building.

It was small and shabby, with peeling paint, rusted gutters and a large cracked window showing a large room with a staircase tucked off to one side, facing the road.

"It's an old house that needs to be bulldozed," she commented with a shrug.

"Ahh, look again." He prompted looping his arm through hers and leading Willa onto the small wooden porch. "They don't make them like this anymore. The structure is as sound as the mountain itself. A few alterations, a bit of a facelift, a slap of paint, new windows – obviously, and this would make a lovely first home."

As he lead the way around the side, Willa looked again with fresh eyes. The back of the house led directly into the nursery garden. The rear door was solid wood and didn't budge an inch when she pushed on it. The tiny window was grimy but gave a small glimpse of what looked to be a relatively large kitchen with extremely old appliances gathering spiderwebs. The view of the nursery would be a lovely background while Saskia cooked, she thought.

With an unexpected jolt, Willa suddenly found herself in Daniel's arms, standing on the old corrugated tin porch roof. The sash window groaned as the vampire forced it open and clambered through waving for Willa to follow.

"Upstairs there are three bedrooms, a bathroom and an attic room in the roof space," Dan explained. "Just imagine what you could make of it…"

Willa couldn't help but smile as she moved through the dusty rooms. The hardwood floors were bare and filthy but intact. The bathroom looked to be twice as old as she was, with a rusted sink and bathtub, no shower and a cracked porcelain toilet. All three bedrooms were tiny, not much bigger than a double bed each, grouped around the bathroom. On the staircase landing, a door led to another extremely slim, steep set of stairs leading to the attic. And oh what an attic. The floor space covered the entire footprint of the house, with wood panelling on the walls and a tiny south-facing window under the eaves. It was one big empty space with a single light bulb hung from the ceiling and there was nothing else to see.

"What do you make of it?" Daniel prompted, holding Willa steady as she traversed the stairs back down to the bedrooms.

"What do I make of it? It's a dump… I mean, the bathroom needs redoing completely, not to mention a total kitchen upgrade. I'd make the attic our bedroom, so we'll need some wardrobes in there. Knock this wall out, and this one." She knocked on the crumbling plaster. "Make these two rooms into one, they're too small to use otherwise. But together they'll be the perfect little loungeroom for us. The one over there would be fine for an office, you know, for Lotions and Potions."

A sly smile crept across Daniel's face. That was exactly what he'd seen when Dornan had mentioned the decrepit building.

"And downstairs, the whole front room would make the perfect shopfront. We can put a door at the bottom of the stairs to keep the customers out. If we set the kitchen area up just right, Sass could still bake whatever she wants plus I can cook up stock for the store. And we wouldn't need storage space as we do now. We'll have a whole shop to put things in…"

Her voice trailed off as the fantasy faded and reality hit Willa in the form of the large glass window facing the road. Facing north. Straight into what during the day, would be the full force of the Australian sun.

"It would never work Dan… The sun. The windows. Saskia can't live here. That's never going to be her kitchen. There are three windows in what would be our lounge room alone… It's so lovely. It's a dump. A tragic mess but I can see how lovely it could be – for a 'normal' person. But not for us. Not for Sass."

Daniel smiled wildly crossing to the cracked window.

"That's the easiest part of all Willa. This is glass, we can just smash it and replace it. You know, one of the things about being as old as I am. I have amassed buckets and buckets of money over the centuries. Money that I've invested in companies that create new technology… Any house can be made vampire proof if your family owns the company that makes UV proof, vampire friendly windows."

Willa spun and threw herself on him with a squeal.

"Really? You can make the windows vampire safe? Truly? I can do the rest but the vampire proofing was beyond me."

Daniel laughed with an enthusiastic nod.

"You make it how you see it and I'll provide whatever windows you desire. I also happen to know that a café is going to be built next door by a local kangaroo shifter, together with the nursery you should have no lack of customers to your shop."

"So, do you happen to know who the current owner is? And if they'd be willing to sell?"

Willas eyes sparkled with anticipation, imaging Saskias reaction to what seemed to be the perfect resolution to all of their problems.

"You're in luck there Willa. Dornan, the Fae who owns the nursery, owns this house. Unfortunately, he's not wanting to sell... Though he is very intent on giving it to you and Saskia free and clear. He believes that it's his duty to ensure our community is happy and thriving and apparently, your owning the house is important to that. He already has the papers drawn up..."

To Daniels shock, Willa burst into heaving sobs.

"This is so perfect. I can't believe it. Wait till Saskia finds out… Oh, wait! Dan, I have another idea… Don't tell Sass a thing. NOT ONE WORD."

CHAPTER 13

"Can I open my eyes yet babe? This is just too weird, you know that right?"

Despite being led along by Willa with her eyes closed, Saskia couldn't help but smile. Whatever the surprise Willa had for her, it had her positively giddy all day and Saskia couldn't help but catch just a smidge of Willa's cheer.

Then again, she'd been oddly buoyant for months now. Whatever secret Willa kept, and Saskia knew full well that she was keeping one; something BIG from her. It was obviously something good if Willa's recent mood was any indication. Willas chipper attitude had even rubbed off on the rest of their family, with Hayden, Daniel and Klaus being on their best behaviour recently. Or maybe that was owing more to her own increasingly assertive attitude towards their home and how best for them to all live together without attracting rodents or public sex shows.

"Almost there love… You're gonna love this! I just know it."

Saskia could feel Willa hopping from foot to foot, gravel crunching beneath her. They'd been walking downhill for the last 15 minutes after leaving their own house and joining the bitumen road, that much Saskia could tell. So they must be somewhere around the nursery by now.

"Ok. Stop here. Hang on, let me just turn you… Yep there. Ok, keep your eyes closed… Now when I say, you can open them. Got it? Not till I say. I want this to be perfect."

Willas voice wasn't right beside her now but it still wasn't far off. Saskia could hear the faint twits of bats that flew overhead, a low creak, shuffling feet and Willa's racing heart. It usually didn't pound like that unless they were in bed.

"Ok, open your eyes and see babe."

A few steps away, Willa stood with a giant, excited smile, on the wooden porch of a quaint little building right beside the entry to the Fae nursery.

"Ta daaa!"

Saskia's confusion cleared as her wife stepped aside to display a large window bearing the words 'Lotions and Potions – Apothecary

"Willa! You got your own shop? Oh my god, this is so brilliant. Why didn't you tell me?"

Saskia was on the porch with Willa wrapped in her arms before Willa even realized she'd moved.

"No babe. I mean yes. We've got our own shop. What your's is mine and what's mine is yours. Joined. One life, one soul. Remember. But no. It's not just a shop…"

Tugging Saskia's hand, Willa dragged her through the shopfront to a door blocking the rest of the building from view. Saskia dug in her heels, her eyes flying around the room taking in the bare shelves, the antique-looking cash register sitting on a wood-topped cabinet. The old-style wall sconces bathed the room in a golden light. Until Willa threw open the door and Saskia stepped into the most darling kitchen she'd ever seen. The solid wood benchtops went on for days, backed by a colourful mosaic of tiny tiles. An oversized double door refrigerator stood in a corner between a door leading outside and a small window that looked over the flowering nursery garden. Between the interior and exterior leading doors was a small café table, waiting set for two. The far wall held a large porcelain farmhouse sink and a large old fashioned iron cooker complete with a double oven and four massive hotplates. At first glance, the cooker could be mistaken for an antique, if not for the bright, royal purple colour.

Willa pressed against Saskia's back, embracing her silent wife as she took in the kitchen before them.

"Welcome home…" she whispered.

"Welcome? What?" Saskia queried stepping out of Willa's embrace.

"Home, my love. Our new home. We both agreed we needed to get our own place. So, I did... Do you like it? I got that oven you're always drooling over. Well, the same model anyway, the cream one was just so boring so I figured you wouldn't mind a little Willa flair. The fridge is a his and hers. One side to fill with food for you to play with. And one side for me to keep my ingredients for brewing in. There's more than enough bench space for us both and with the shop out the front, I won't have stuff piling up and getting in your way, anyway."

Saskia stood frozen. Her wide eyes darting from the cabinets to the sink, to the cooker of her dreams and back to Willa.

"Our house? This is our house? How is this our house? Why is this our house? Willa? This is our house?"

Willa nodded, smiling gleefully, taking Saskia's hand leading her to the staircase that was tucked into the alcove between the benchtops and the door leading to the shop.

"So the night we had the family meeting... Remember? Months ago, when you laid down the law to the others and we discussed our living situation? Well, while you were cracking the domestic whip, Daniel brought me here. The place was a total wreck and at first, I suggested he bulldoze it. But then I took another look and I realized how wonderful it could be with a little work. Klaus and Daniel helped with the heavy lifting and wall bashing and Hayden was an expert in fitting out the shop. We've been working on it for almost six months. It was slow going because, well you know – the whole vampire thing. Not surprisingly, it's difficult to find plumbers and electricians who are willing to work at night. So I supervised the work that had to happen during the daytime, and the guys did the construction after the theatre closed at night… What do you think?"

Willa opened her arms, presenting the cosy lounge room, furnished sparsely with only a sectional couch.

"We went with neutral colours for the walls and just oiled the floors. I figured you'd want to put your own stamp on it. That room is the office, I decided I'd rather be up here with you doing the books and stuff than downstairs in the shop. And up here… Watch your step, they're kinda steep. Up here is our room… What do you think?"

Saskia gasped. How is it that after all this time, her wife still held the ability to make her so overwhelmed with love that she wanted to cry? If she were still capable.

The room was massive. Where the lighting could have been quite dim owing to the only window being so tiny, the room appeared bright and airy, owing to the pale vanilla walls and ceiling, the naturally oiled wood on the floors and the soft cream linens covering the queen-sized bed. The only splash of colour in the whole room was Saskia's beloved chaise situated beneath the small window.

"How did that get here?" She asked. "I was just sitting on it back home. Literally. I was sitting on it, I stood up, and you brought me here…"

"Klaus" Willa giggled. "As soon as we were out the door, he ran it down here for me. Why do you think I made you walk so slowly? I had to give him time to beat us here."

Saskia rolled her eyes, and people thought vampires were aloof and didn't care…

"Willa, I love it. The whole place is so beautiful. It's just the sort of home I dreamed of when I was human. I never wanted a big manor house with staff and a wealthy husband. I wanted this, a comfortable home with someone who loves me for more than my parents' name. It's so perfect. And I love the store. It's just what Lotions and Potions needs. I just wish I could be here with you."

Willa's face fell.

"But it's our home. I made it just for us. Where else would you be?"

"Darling, look around. Even that tiny window is will let in the sun. I can't live here. I can't help you in the shop. I can't cook for you in that fabulous kitchen. The windows. In a few hours, I have to go back to the family house…"

Willa grasped Saskia and pressed her lips to her plump, ruby lips.

"That's the best part," she murmured, sucking firmly on Saskia's bottom lip. "Did you know that Daniel invests his money?"

Nodding, Saskia crowded Willa back towards the beautiful bed. She may not be able to live here, but she had at least a few hours to 'play house' before sunrise.

"Did you know that one of those companies is the one that makes the vampire safe windows, like the one back at the cave house? Every pane of glass in this entire house is UV filtering and completely vampire safe."

Saskia paused, pulling away fractionally from Willa's ministrations.

"Vampire safe glass? All of it? Even the shop and the doors, and everything?"

Willas smug, satisfied smile was all the confirmation she needed.

"Well, in that case, let"s make ourselves at home..." glancing over her shoulder Saskia kicked the door closed as she pushed Willa gently onto the bed.

"Guys? If you're still here... Fuck off!" Saskia yelled as Willa's t-shirt flew across the room in two pieces.

"Ok, so if you have the shop now, what happens with all the other stores you're supplying?"

Saskia sat cross-legged on the floor behind the counter sorting through the myriad of jars and bottles that Willa had already stockpiled for the store while Willa began arranging the shelves into categories. Saskia still couldn't believe that she was sitting here. On the floor of Willa's shop. In their very own home. In the middle of the day. Honestly, while she'd have loved to be arranging and lining all those jars and boxes just so, the bright sunlight outside gave her pause despite both Willa and Daniels reassurances that the glass in the large store window was the same if not better than that which made up the front wall of their family home.

After two days of appreciating her new home and making plans to personalize the décor, she and Willa had returned to the cave house just long enough for them to pack all their clothes and personal belongings up and for the rest of the family to load the Lotions and Potions stockpile into the boot and backseat of Willa's car. Willa had insisted that Saskia take care of their personal unpacking, safe inside the house, while she made the dozens of trips to unload the boxes from the car in the hot sunshine.

"Well, I haven't just spent that last six months building our home you know. I've been working on our shop as well. I've been fazing most of the other stores out slowly and all the labels and packaging over the past few months have had the details of our new location."

Willa shrugged as though it was no big deal, but Saskia couldn't believe that her somewhat flighty wife who regularly forgot where she left her coffee in the morning, had such a shrewd business mind.

"I kept a few little boutiques on. None here on the mountain, but there are a few in the city that were eager to pay a premium for a few exclusive potions. They also have a list of the entire range we'll be selling here and I've promised to supply a special limited edition soap twice a year. Daniel says it's a good business plan."

Willa turned and joined Saskia on the floor entwining their fingers and kissing her lightly.

"Babe? Why do you keep referring to Lotions and Potions as my store? You've been cooking up creams with me for years and your nose for shampoo and soap scents is much more refined than mine. We wouldn't even have a business if it wasn't' for you. Besides, what better advertisement for our skincare than your immaculate face. This is just as much your store as it is mine."

Saskia absently stroked the pale burn scar on the back of Willa's hand. The same one she'd noticed all those years ago. She now knew Willa had gotten it a few months before they'd met, cooking up some wattle soap in her kitchen.

"I still don't understand how it can be, sweetie. I mean, I'm happy to help you make stock and work behind the scenes and all. But I can't be out here during the day.

Even with our special sun-safe glass. Think about it Willa, every time a customer comes through the door, the glass seal is broken and the sun shines in. Now call me pessimistic, but I'm guessing a crispy fried vampire is not the 'face of the business' that will inspire purchases."

Willa burst out laughing, apparently she'd become a little too distracted when she'd been championing the benefits of their home and forgotten one important key.

"I've got that covered babe. I know I haven't practised my craft recently but my magic is stronger than ever. Remember at our wedding, Lord Gruphig said that by joining our lives, our blood, it wouldn't just link our lives and souls, our magic would strengthen each others? Well, I used some of that super-duper magic and created a protective net over our home. When we finished all the building work, I charged a bunch of quartz crystals with an encantation during the new moon and then buried them all around the outside of the house. Those crystals are millions of years old and are more powerful than any others. As long as they remain, this building is safe. The glass in the windows is stronger, it can never break, never let the sun in, when the door is open the protection stays in place. Hell, you could probably even stand on the porch for a minute or two… Though I really, really, don't want you to try it. What I'm saying babe, is that I've got you."

Pulling Saskia into an embrace Willa stroked the worry lines from her face.

"You supported me when my parents didn't want me. You supported me when I quit my job and started Lotions. You've supported me in every way possible over all these years, given me more than you could ever realise. This is something I could give you. Something you've always wanted. A 'normal' life. Plus I get the bonus of working with my lovely wife if she wants the job. Of course, you're welcome to stay home and be a kept woman but if you want to try your hand at retail... Well, it's not only safe for you, but I'd love it."

"You cast a spell? Over the entire building? For me?"

Saskia could barely find her voice, as emotions she'd never felt before bubbled up inside her. Slowly very slowly, she reached out a hand, clearing the counter towards the light coming through the glass window.

"No matter what, the sun can never get me? I can work here? Meet real people? Be a normal person? Working during the day and loving my woman at night?"

Again Willa nodded, loving Saskias amazement.

"I love you so much babe" Saskia whispered as her voice finally cracked. "I'd love to work in OUR store with you. On one condition... I get to make the display under the counter, I've got a really great idea."

CHAPTER 14

"Love, I'm thinking we should just stay closed this weekend. It's supposed to be a scorcher, they reckon over 40. There won't be many tourists venturing out of their aircon and up the mountain, so I vote we do the same."

Saskia called through the open door to Willa. Though they did a solid business all week through, the weekend was usually their busiest time, what with tourists coming up the mountain. But Lotions and Potions had been going strong for years now and they wouldn't be hurt by closing for a few days. Besides, it would give them a chance to stocktake, relax, enjoy some time together... Just the two of them. They could spend all day in bed if they wanted. Saskia could cook up a few treats and Willa could use some of that lavender honey and strawberry lotion that she'd made for their wedding and had been rationing ever since. Yes, a weekend off to eat, drink and be merry sounded pretty damn good.

Willa leaned her head out and took in her wife, sitting cross-legged on the floor behind the counter. Even after all the years, safe in the knowledge that she was perfectly protected from the sun within their home, that spot was still her favourite spot in the shop. Of course, it helped that the counter beneath the cash register held her precious collection. Willa knew, there was nothing Saskia found more relaxing (that didn't involve food and Willa herself) than sitting on the floor after closing and dusting the dozens of tiny, jewel-coloured perfume bottles she'd gathered over her long life.

"Sounds good to me my love. I agree, I doubt many will venture far from their aircon. All week it's been slower than usual in here and it's only going to get hotter over the next few days."

Willa was already imagining what they could do with their weekend off. She knew it would include a bite to eat or two and that idea thrilled her no end. There was nothing that turned her on more in life than the feel of her wifes' fangs piercing her skin unless it was when Saskia tried to resist and Willa managed to breach her control.

Suddenly an unwelcome thought popped into her head.

"Oh honey, I almost forgot. I have to run down to the lavender farm in Garfield tomorrow and pick up our order. Their truck's broken down and we're completely out. It'll only take a few hours and the car aircon should keep me and the plants cool enough."

Saskia pouted, her plump lips teasing Willa.

"You mean you're going to leave me here all alone to fend for myself? What if something happens? What if a marauding kangaroo pack stages a take over in the village? What if a bunyip wants to buy bubble bath?"

Willa giggled, kissing Saskias crestfallen face.

"Oh my god, dramatic much? I'm sure you'll live. It's only a few hours love and the shop will be closed remember? Hell, you lived for over a century without me, so you'll be fine while I pick up supplies. Maybe you can cook me up something special, something cool and full of strawberries? Then, we can soak in the tub, and I don't think we've christened the new rug in the office. You know the rules about new furnishings…"

Saskia sighed against Willa's teasing lips and then collapsed dramatically back onto the floor.

"I guess I'll just have to struggle through. After all, what's the worse that can happen?"

The car lurched suddenly onto the soft shoulder of the road as a blinding light flashed through her mind, stealing Willa's sight momentarily. Slowing, she came to a shuddering stop, grasping her head and gulping great lungs full of air.

As the searing flash cleared, the unease she'd felt all day ramped into full-on dread. A sense of foreboding the like of which she'd never felt before and was unable to explain was rising. Something dreadful was coming. Sucking in a slow, deep breath Willa closed her eyes and struggled to centre herself. Her heart raced, so hard, so fast. Without even realizing she began to quietly chant over and over. The temperature in the car rose quickly without the aircon blasting. Willa could feel sweat begin to bead on her skin. Even through her closed lids, she sensed the light draining from the world. Casting her gaze about, the day had ended so suddenly. Her watch reassured her that it was only 3 in the afternoon but the twilight indicated the time being so much later. Ahead a thick black cloud obscured a normally clear view of the mountain. The cars moving past on the highway, the fields and trees only metres away beside the road... Everything was becoming shrouded in thick smoke. Grey ash fell like snow coating her car.

The dry heat burned her skin. It almost felt as though it was peeling away, scorched layer by layer. Her chant lost, Willa panted hard and fast, the blood in her veins boiled, bringing new heat to her tortured body. The pain was so overwhelming, so much so that she didn't even notice when the heat flowing through her body turned from fiery hot to frigid.

An icy knife pierced her heart, taking the last of her breath away. As the shard of ice twisted and turned, digging further, pain tore through Willa, consuming all thought. Somehow she knew, she understood without explanation that magic was afoot and would destroy her this day.

Her heart stuttered, stopped and hiccuped to beat again. Forcing the ice through her body as she was torn apart layer by layer, piece by piece. Tears evaporated before they hit her cheeks as her eyes locked on where her mountain should be. Willa was filled with horror as she felt her life slipping away. She could feel her body burning, turning to ash to be scattered by the hot wind. The shard of ice twisted once more inside her chest, stopping her heart for eternity.

An unearthly shriek tore through her. A sound she'd never heard before, she'd never made before and one she hoped she would never hear again. It was the sound of life obliterated, a broken wail of unfiltered pain.

"Sassy! Sasss-eeee!"

The darkness overtook Willa, erasing the world and everything in it as her heart began to beat again with the vigour of newborn life.

CHAPTER 15

Willa hung her head, yet another dead end. Yet another nail in the coffin that was her life. Her death. Her families death, her communities death. Saskia's death. And Willa's never-ending afterlife. It had been months since the fire had torn through her mountain erasing her community. She knew that her Sassy was gone. Everyone was gone. There were no more Fae. No shifters roaming the bush. No trolls, no gnomes… No vampires.

Willa hadn't realized the devastation at the time, all she felt was Saskia. She'd been warned. She knew there were risks, but she'd never conceived that their blessing would become such a curse as this. All magic came with a price and now she was paying. As far as she knew, she was the last witch standing and in all honesty, she wasn't even that anymore.

Her mind spoke the truth over and over and yet her heart refused to accept. She could still feel Saskia's essence running through her with every heartbeat. The heart that believed Saskia was alive, that somehow she'd survived when no one else had. Tried to convince her mind that her beloved was out there somewhere. Her damn heart tortured her nightly.

It had been many months now, she's accepted what she'd become. At first, she'd been frantic, searching every inch of the mountain for some sign of those that she loved. Of those that she'd lost. Day after day, she'd combed through the wreckage of the cottage, finding only charred wood and ash. Until the moment her fingers had curled around a crystal buried by debris. It was grey and lifeless and cracked through the centre by the heat. The glow of the magic that it had held was extinguished now, and along with it their wedding blessing and Saskia's eternal life. Her fist had tightened around the useless chunk of minerals and as she shrieked her pain she beat it on the solid slab until it was a small pile of glittering dust. The blessing had indeed become her curse.

With her body turned to ash, Saskia's afterlife still flowed through Willa. Overwhelming her own magic with centuries of power. She no longer needed to eat, to sleep, to go through any of the small, mundane actions that made up the human day. Saskia's power and her Wiccan powers fought for space within the weary shell that was her body, twisting and changing all that she was. And then a blessed moment of peace would descend, a few scant days when the moon was full, she would find herself again within the kaleidoscope of changing magic. It was in those paltry hours that she would cry. When she could feel pain. When she could put words to it and truly grieve. Though as much as she wished she could escape into fantasy, even in the few hours sleep she managed it pursued her. Her wondrous dreams of Saskia and their happy life together had disappeared. Erased by the flames as surely as her beloved had been. There was only so much space within one little Wiccan soul, and it seemed that it was all occupied with the magic of her lost loved ones, leaving no room for dreams or escapes of the imagination. She had dreamed her final dream, sitting by the side of the road, when she'd closed her eyes and burned in the sun and the fire with Saskia. Her days of happy dreaming had ended with that nightmare.

It was in those moments when the moon was full that she felt her witch rise. She visited communities far from the mountain, read books, spoke with shamans and elders. Those were the days she chanted and begged the goddesses and the very universe itself for clarity. For an explanation, a reason why they all had to die. For an answer as to why the fire had not succumbed to the entire supernatural communities combined magic. For the answer as to what she had become.

The warring magic within her was a testament that she was neither a witch nor was she vampire. With the daylight, she was overcome by Saskia's desire to bake. All she wanted was to cook and decorate and visit flea markets to find unique furnishings to create a special place all of her own. As the sun dropped below the horizon, creating that same shadowed light that had covered the mountain in the middle of that fateful day, Willa's thoughts of cushions, candles and pastry were ripped from her mind along with all consciousness. All that remained was her pain as she wandered the mountains each night, her voice raw and cracked as it poured from her throat in an unearthly shriek. A call to the dead. A call to those left living. A call that went unanswered night after night. And yet she remained compelled, no matter that her human self had accepted that she alone had survived – the magic trapped within her was compelled to search, to call and never to find.

Frozen in time, she faced an eternity of wailing. Immortality stretched before her, such was the life of the wailing woman. The life of a banshee.

She knew what she had become, and the blessing had indeed become a curse, the price that had to be paid.

THE END

MORE JAKKI FRANCES READS….

Destroying Laura

Easily Distracted By Camels

Firestorm

(Bigelow Bay series)

It's Safer

It's Complicated

Keeping Control

(Mountain Magic series)

Fairy Tale

Marsupial Muttering

For all the news and the crazy that's in my head, find me at:

www.jakkifrancesauthor.com

www.facebook.com/jakkifrances

www.instagram.com/jakkifrancesauthor